Return to
CHESHIRE BAY

USA TODAY BESTSELLING AUTHOR

H.M. SHANDER

Return to Cheshire Bay

Published by H.M. Shander Publishing
Copyright 2021 H.M. Shander

Cover Design: Eleanor Lloyd-Jones @ Shower of Schmidt Designs
Editing: PWA & IDIM Editorial
Shander, H.M., 1975—Return to Cheshire Bay

Dedicated to a summer of broken dreams,
afternoons spent int the backyard
under the red umbrella with an iced coffee in hand.
And to the Squirrels — Duncan & Carlos and their kids,
Cedar, George & Rusty

Table of Contents

Chapter One

Three months.

Ninety-one days exact to figure out what the hell I needed, and the clock was ticking.

Time wasn't a disposable luxury anymore, and putting my high-rise city life on hold to escape to my childhood beach home in the small-town of Cheshire Bay was the only thing I had control over. For the time being.

It was time to clear away the cobwebs, both figurative and literal.

It was high time I found myself.

Back in my wild teenage years, Cheshire Bay had given me the best summers of my life. Endless beach parties. Zero boundaries. No parental involvement. I had even been the reigning Miss Cheshire Bay my last summer here, some twelve years ago.

Until…

That horrible incident everyone blamed me for.

Had they forgotten? Oh, who am I kidding? Small

towns talk and they never forget. Never. But what choice did I have in coming back?

In three months, I was going to have a serious cash flow problem. The quickest way to solve that problem was to update and sell the beach home, long neglected since Mom's death. My sister wanted nothing to do with it, and Dad had willed it to me to do with it as I pleased. Money trumped roots, and besides, I needed the cash.

As the sun dipped into the Pacific Ocean, the air around me cooled enough to warrant needing a light sweater. Wiping away the small stream of tears, I rose from the postcard perfect beach and dusted off my butt and legs, ambling up to the weathered porch stretching across the back of the house, and into a kitchen barely big enough for a family.

After slipping my oversized Under Armour hoodie on, I grabbed a mug of steaming apple cider tea and pulled myself up onto the wide ledge running along the deck. Leaning against one of the posts, vacantly staring out into the twilight, I was ready to find the first star of the night. A cool evening breeze circled the coastline, and the occasional shudder ruffled my wisps of hair.

The lights in the house next door flickered on and an unfamiliar shape walked through the kitchen. It was lit up enough inside to see the walls were a muted shade of mint and the cabinetry was as white as snow. The man inside walked back and forth, and finally emerged onto his deck with a long neck bottle of beer, sitting in the darkened shadows.

Years ago, back when I was a crazy, stupid teenager, that house used to occupy the Morris family; a typical mom-dad-two-kids deal. Like us, and just about everyone on this strip, they were summer families – arriving right after school finished and leaving September long weekend. I never knew where they went after closing up, and never cared to ask, they were just other kids to play with when we were here. Until I became too cool to hang out with dorks and preferred the company of bad boys. Or bad men as it sometimes came to be.

The memories flittered away as I gazed intently upon my neighbour. He most definitely wasn't Mr. Morris, who last time I saw was an older father and certainly would not be moving with such speed. And based on the outline, it wasn't either of the two boys who were gangly, paper thin, and maybe weighed a hundred pounds soaking wet. Perhaps, when the economy took its nasty turn, the Morris family sold, and a new occupant moved in. It had happened before. Not all on this section of the beach were lifetime owners anymore. Just me and a few of the others. At least, last I'd heard.

Oh well.

Tomorrow in the fresh light, after ensuring I was

presentable, I'd go over and introduce myself. If I was going to be here a while, may as well be the neighbourly one. Besides my house had been unoccupied for so long, seeing life within it may set off alarm bells.

I listened to the waves caressing the shoreline as I inhaled nice deep breaths of air hinted with the apple cinnamon scent from my tea. Every breath I took, my shoulders fell, and I melted into the pillar. It was too easy to give into it all.

The deep staccato beats from Darth Vader's theme blared out of my phone, echoing off the wood, and I jumped, tossing my hands out to the side. In a rush to rebalance, I knocked my mug clear off the edge where it landed with a crashing crack and the sound of liquid spraying about.

"Damn it, Parker."

Why was my ex-boyfriend calling? What the hell did he need? Didn't he get everything he wanted when he walked out on me?

The spicy scent drifted in the air. The shards of ceramic. Tea everywhere. Shit.

My feet were naked, and I wasn't about to step anywhere until I could see properly, so I rolled off the ledge and jumped into the sand six feet below. Butterflies swirled in my gut.

"Who's there?" The gruff voice called over the

darkness.

"Shit. Shit. Shit." I swore under my breath. Not the perfect way to introduce myself to the neighbour. "Sorry. I live here and when my phone rang, I knocked my tea off. Give me a sec."

I walked up the stairs and stayed as far away as possible from where I predicted the mug had shattered, and stretching out my step, I used my toes to grip the edge of the doorframe. Once inside, I slipped into my shoes and flicked on the porch light, pinching my eyes closed to the brightness.

After a second or two when I was no longer blind, I grabbed for the broom and greeted the lack of a mess I was expecting.

"Everything okay?" The male voice called out with concern lacing his words.

I bent down, back to my neighbour, and picked up the mug, spying a hairline crack but nothing more. "Yeah. Amazingly enough, it's all good."

In the house, I trashed the old cup, while also turning on the under the cabinets lights to give a muted glow to the area and switched off the harsh deck light outside – it was bright enough to act like a lighthouse beacon.

I headed over to the far end of the patio, closest to my neighbour's. "I was going to wait until tomorrow to introduce myself, but since I've ruined the quiet vibe of the evening, may as well do it now."

"I think Darth Vader can take the rap."

A slight chuckle rolled out of me, pleased he knew the familiarity of the musical clip. "Yeah, we can totally blame him. I'm Lily, by the way."

"Lily, as in Lily Baker?"

My jaw dropped. Baker was a name I hadn't used in years. At least not professionally. That name belonged to a wild child, and clearly, this person remembered the rebellious teenager who believed she was invincible.

The weakest response rolled out. "None other."

"Wow. You sure grew up."

Wish I could say the same about him as neither his voice nor his shape was at all familiar. I took a chance. "Mr. Morris?" But it couldn't be. This voice was younger, with a sexy undercurrent to it.

A deep laugh filled the air. "Only at doctor's appointments." His feet shuffled across his wooden deck. "Don't you recognize me?" The patter of feet faded into the sand, and his shadow made his way in my direction, into the edge of the light. "You still don't know who I am, do you?"

I stared, shaking with disbelief. "How can I? You're still in the shadows."

The man before me was fully filled out and quite

tall, something neither of the Morris boys had ever been. As he fully entered the light, I gasped as the boy had become a man. And damn, a good-looking one at that too. Long gone was the baby-faced, pimple-filled, gangly teenaged boy.

Having a 50/50 shot between the brothers, I took a gamble. "Landon?" He was the baby, a year younger than me, and the one I'd often thought was less geeky.

"No," his voice fell in disappointment, something I related to when people found out it was me and not my goody-two-shoes sister. "Just Eric."

Ohmygod. *Just Eric* was a full-fledged hottie. A caterpillar who'd burst out of his cocoon into a handsome, buff butterfly. Enough to cause my own in the pit of my stomach to swirl in excitement over seeing him after all these years.

"Mona here too?"

"No, she couldn't make it." Couldn't be bothered was more like it, even if she wouldn't let the place go. But it wasn't up to her to decide anymore.

"Cool. Can I come up? It'd be great to catch up."

"Sure, I'd like that."

He stepped onto my deck and the sight of him up close made my jaw fall and my heart responded with an uptick in speed. *Just Eric* had sprouted a good twelve inches since the last time I'd seen him and easily stood over six feet tall. "So… who's the Star Wars fan?"

"Me. Totally me." Assigning a fitting John Williams score to my top ten callers was fun. Giving Parker the Sith Lord theme was even better, especially since he was a slave to his own uncontrollable emotions.

"Who's the Darth Vader for?"

"No one important." Because he made it that way. Ended our relationship without warning because the terms and conditions had changed, and he wasn't onboard with any of it.

Eric seemed to have sensed my tone and eased away from the inquiry. He leaned on the edge of the deck, his leg muscles tight beneath his shorts. "You back for a couple of weeks?"

"Actually, just like the good ole days, I'll be here all summer. I think." Hadn't worked through all the details completely, but it sounded good to say it regardless, and I hoped the mock confidence rolled out.

A little flutter took flight in my gut as a wanderlust expression filled his handsome face. It was still hard to believe a gawky teenager like he'd been, was now a stunningly gorgeous guy.

"You here for the summer too?"

"Nah, I live here year-round."

"Wow, really?" I couldn't imagine the seaside summer village being very busy during the cool, winter months.

"I work at the airport."

"You're a pilot?" I tried to hide the pitch at the end of my question but was sure I failed miserably.

"Charter flights, mostly around the island." There was a twinkle in his voice along with a hint of pride. "A life-long dream. Sort of. I'm not flying the big jumbo jets, but I'm still taking to the skies."

Not only had he sprouted, but he'd figuratively earned his wings.

Impressive.

"Well, there's lots to see and do on the island. I'm sure the tourists love it." At least I hoped the list of things to do had expanded. All I ever did as a teenager was drink and smoke too much weed on the beaches while giving into my carnal desires.

"Fair bit. I do the occasional run to YVR." Airport code for Vancouver. "So, if you ever need anything from your place while you're here, gimme a holler. I can fly you over. Less than an hour gate to gate."

That would be a first - being shuttled around by a kid who was uber annoying and a giant pain in the ass. Whenever we were on the beach, him and Landon would follow my friends and me around like pathetic pitiful puppies. If I knew then he'd turn out to be a nice guy, maybe I would've been nicer to him.

Darth Vader's march sounded out again, and I quickly yanked my phone off the ledge, silencing it and flipping it face down. Parker could wait–forever–for all I cared. That ship had sailed.

"Tomorrow night, would you be interested in having supper? We can catch up." He kicked at the weathered floor of my deck and checked out the time on his watch. "I'd invite you out tonight, but I'm going to a friend's and…"

"No, no, that's okay, honestly. Tomorrow works or even the next day too. I'm kind of exhausted anyway and need to catch up on my sleep." I hadn't had a full night's rest in a month, and especially not over the last week.

"Perfect, tomorrow it's a date, and I'll come pick you up." With a quick wave, he walked across the beach between us and disappeared into his home.

A date? I laughed. As if. I wasn't back in Cheshire Bay to relive my glory days; I was here to figure out my life.

I had three months to get my affairs in order - clean up the beach house, ready it for sale, and prepare for a new me and a new life. Dates with the cute guy next door were not on the agenda and would never be.

I gave my belly a rub, and a gentle kick greeted my hand.

Three months to go.

Chapter Two

"Whatcha doing?" Eric asked, popping his head out his car as he pulled up in front of his place.

I lifted a can of paint from the rear of my Jeep and waved it in front of me. "Renovating."

He walked over and retrieved a couple bags of supplies and the other two cans of paint, following me into the house. "Sorry I didn't come and grab you for our supper date the other night. An emergency popped up with a friend, and by time I got back here your lights were all off."

"It's all good, I promise."

I hadn't expected much anyway. Figured he blew me off like I had him so many times before. Besides, this wasn't the right time in my life for a date-date. A friendly coffee, as wonderful as the thought was, was almost too much to handle. Especially since being back in the bay area.

"I've been working more with the incoming tourists."

"Eric," I paused and rifled through the bag of supplies sitting on the kitchen island. "Trust me, it's okay." Right at the bottom was the package of plastic tarps I needed.

A look of relief tugged his shoulders downward and pushed a smile into his cheeks. "Whew." He mocked wiping his brow and turned to take in the change of scenery. "Wow." A high-pitched whistle blew through his lips. "You've totally changed the looks of this place."

I narrowed my eyes. As far as I remembered, I'd never invited him over, so how would he know?

He set a paint can down on the floor. "On occasion I'd pop over and make sure everything was okay – no water lines busted, that kind of thing. Your dad hired me to keep an eye on the place. By the way, is he coming by at all? I'd like to touch base with him."

I froze in the spot for a heartbeat and swallowed down a rapidly forming lump. "No, he's not coming." Quickly, I averted my gaze.

"Ah, well, too bad." He ran his fingers through his hair. "This looks amazing, and you've given it a modern spin. I like it."

"Excuse its current disaster though."

Normally, I was a neat and tidy person, but being

here, there was the overwhelming urge to declutter, clean and repaint, and the result was a temporary pigsty. Sure, the walls were freshly painted in an interesting choice of grey, which wasn't my first pick, but the floors were littered in nightmare of weathered books, knickknacks and items that desperately needed to never see the light of day again.

"I promise, it's not permanent. I have big plans for this space." I lifted the can of paint at Eric's feet, twisting and debating where precisely to put it.

The main floorplan was open concept, and the sitting area only had three walls. One had an empty, but unpainted, bookcase from the 1950's that took up the length of the wall and filled three-quarters of the height. The other two walls were half windows; one gazing out to green hilly seaside, and the other stared out onto the covered deck which faced the ocean. Painting those two walls had been easy. It was the bookcase wall providing some challenges since it was firmly attached to the wall and I couldn't just slap a paint roller on it and be done. The wall needed to be painted, as did the bookcase, but I wasn't sure if it should match the wall, or something different to make it pop. While I figured it out (and waited for a call from my best friend and interior decorator), I'd painted the kitchen but without her returning my call, I'd started painting the upstairs. And that's when I ran out of supplies.

"Like everything else in my life, it was time for a change." I set the heavy can down with a thud and leaned back against the counter, forgetting for the briefest of heartbeats that Eric was here. And he didn't know all the things. Had I thought it through, I would've rested in a way that didn't speak volumes and announced my condition.

Eric's eyes sailed over my body and focused, like everyone else had since my return, on my slightly protruding bump.

I fluffed my shirt and sighed. There was no point in hiding it, he was going to notice it soon enough and in a small town everyone seemed to know everyone else's business, like it or not. Perhaps, if I came clean first, it would put to rest the rumours that eventually rose from the mistruths. Even if my reasons for moving here hadn't yet become clear to me, there was no point in withholding the facts.

"Yep, I'm pregnant. Due September fourteenth to be exact." I gave the bump a rub. "My twenty-two-year-old man-child of a boyfriend said he wasn't ready for a baby, and after emptying his drawer in my apartment, he's out of the picture. Dad had a heart attack just before Easter, but the damage was too much, and he passed away a couple of months ago. Then there's my lovely sister who refuses to talk to me because she's the oldest and she was supposed to have kids first. Her raging jealousy hit epic levels because I got *knocked up,* and she's been trying for six years to have children."

Despite the silent staring and slack jaw look, I remained on my mission of airing my dirty laundry and let the words continue to spew. "Oh, right. To add insult to injury, the company I worked for was just bought out by a huge Asian firm, so I received a nice little buyout package, but I'm effectively jobless. Thankfully the Wi-Fi here isn't atrocious, and I can build my own company to help cover the bills while I figure out what the hell I'm doing." I dropped my hands to the side and breathed out. Relief wasn't even the right word to express the emotions that fell like a waterfall. It was refreshing to spill it all. "Imagine my surprise. I'm thirty years old and starting my life over, and it's not quite how I planned. Not even close."

Eric pulled out a kitchen stool and sat with a thump. "That was a lot of information in thirty seconds." He wiped a hand across his forehead.

"Can I get you something to drink?" Without waiting for an answer, I filled a glass with water and handed it to him.

He gulped it all down. To his credit, he seemed to be handling the news much better than Dad had, and way better than Parker. "You're telling me you're all alone in this?" His gazed slowly dropped to my slight bump.

"Pretty much."

"And your dad, he's… he died?" The smidgen of hurt was unmistakable.

My voice softened. "Yeah. Had I known you were taking care of the place, I would've let you know. There was nothing in his journals that mentioned a property caretaker. I just assumed he came out once in a while."

"Damn, I'm really sorry to hear of his passing. I always liked him." His face fell, and somewhere in my heart an ache formed. It seemed Eric was closer to my father than I had been. "And you've moved here for the time being, to kind of sort out your personal situation?"

"For now, yes. I still have my place downtown, but I guess I'll see what becomes of things here." I gave my tummy a rub.

The little one was slowly moving around. Guess the verbal diarrhea pumped my heartbeat and woke someone.

Eric rose and offered me the stool. "You should be the one to sit."

I rolled my eyes. "I'm pregnant, not elderly. I'm fine." Instead, I filled another glass of water, this one for me, and I took a few sips. "Sorry, I didn't mean to dump on you. I forgot how small some towns can be and all the looks I got, especially from the hardware store after they recognized me, they all rubbed me the wrong way."

"Yeah, you look pretty much like how I remembered." He huffed and took another drink of water, walking over to the sink and refilling it. "Sorry about the hardware store. Guess some people never forgot who you are."

I lifted a shoulder and sighed. "Who I *was*."

The joys of small-town life. It was nice being anonymous in the big city. No one knew me, no one knew about my past. Thirteen years distance should've been enough of a gap. Boy, oh boy, was I wrong.

"Where'd you go get your stuff?"

"Stewart Surf."

He rocked side to side. "You probably got hosed."

I laughed and tilted my head back. "Oh, most likely. But it was better than the hardware store here."

The joys of island living included a higher cost of living. However, living on the beach, I wouldn't need as much as I did in the city. Ironic. I finished my water and put my glass into the sink. Grabbing an armful of supplies, I headed upstairs and into my childhood bedroom. It didn't have the amazing view of the Pacific Ocean like the master bedroom, so I was readying it as a guest room.

Eric followed me up and came armed with a can of paint. "You doing all grey up here as well?"

I looked around my former bedroom with the large window easy enough to sneak into, if a certain sister left the window open after I'd climbed up the lattice. "Yeah, think so."

Currently, the room was a sand colour, but it was faded and very dated as the last time it was painted was before Mona was born.

I read the colour on Eric's can. "Give me a sec, I need the other one."

Inside the freshly painted master bedroom was the other open can I needed to finish first. All rooms had undergone a transformation, and yet none of them were even close to being finished. A bad habit of starting projects and not seeing them all the way through, even though I promised myself, this time would be different.

I set Eric's can – the tag called it *Stormy Seas* - along the windowed wall. It was a deeper blue grey. Once I painted the window trim in white, it should have a nice contrast, which was the vision I had for my old room. Some people didn't like the grey palette, but I found it comforting and modern, once I got beyond the initial institutional feel.

"Need some help?"

"Nah. I'll need to wash walls in here first, but I don't mind."

All the personality had been stripped off the walls years ago. The posters had long been taken down, our N'Sync years behind us. There was only a bed and dresser, and I could easily still move those into the centre of the room. I'd managed in the master bedroom on my own.

"I feel like I can't leave you to do this." He

unbuttoned his cuffs, and rolled them up, exposing his taut arms.

Damn. What was it about guys in dress shirts with the sleeves rolled up? I shook away the lustful feelings. It was a sweet gesture on Eric's part to help, but I couldn't accept. "Would you have insisted on helping had you not discovered I was pregnant?"

He looked down and shuffled his feet. "No, I still would've helped."

"Honestly, I'll be fine." I put my hands on my hips. "It'll be therapeutic in a way. Cleaning and changing everything. At least this is a part of my life I have some control over."

He checked his watch. "Fair enough. I can respect that."

Playfully, I swatted his arm - his strong, muscled arm. Damn. "Pretend like I didn't dump my woes on you ten minutes ago about my wildly unhinged life and pretend I'm still a cantankerous and rebellious seventeen-year-old. When my mind is made up, there's not much you can do to change it."

"Sounds like some things haven't changed." A gentle grin formed on his tanned face. "Well, if you don't need me?" He waited, and I shook my head. "Then I should get back to the airport. Just had some time between flights, and I needed to grab something from the house." He walked to the door and hesitated, opening his mouth and closing it just as quick.

I followed him out and walked ahead of him down the stairs. I needed a bucket and my phone for music, wishing I had brought my sound bar. It would've come in handy. "Thanks for the help."

Eric hung by the door, a debate warring on his face, and I couldn't tell if he was perplexed or offended.

I leaned against the frame, stalling as I wasn't ready to let him walk away just yet. The interruption had been pleasant. "Hey, is our section of beach still private?"

"Sure is. Both towns worked to clean up a long stretch of public beaches, including long beach. This way, this stretch of beach remains private to the homeowners."

"Cool."

Years ago, there had been talk about making the beach public property, at least according to Dad. He and a few of the other homeowners must've fought hard to keep it belonging to the residents only.

Eric opened the screen door and stepped on to the front porch. "Tonight." The word hung in the air for a few heartbeats. "Why don't you come over for supper?"

"Supper?" My heart pounded in anticipation.

"You do eat, right?" Up and down, he scanned, that grin of his widening into a mega-watt smile with enough power to launch the butterflies into my gut at high speed.

"I've been known to have a bite here and there." Suddenly, I was fifteen again and the cute boy was asking me out for ice cream. Had my hair not been piled on my head, I may have grabbed a piece and twirled it around my finger while batting my eyes.

"Perfect. I'll have dinner ready for seven. Does that work?" He cocked his head to the side.

"I'll set a timer." I winked. This side of the island was so relaxed, time was meaningless. Always had been.

With a wave, he walked away, and I studied his behind until it was rounding his vehicle. Yep. Time had done wonders for Eric. Did he think the same about me?

Chapter Three

ours later, I had to admit, the change to the guest room was dramatic, and it was the first room in the house to be done. The room looked amazing and with the right accessories, it would be worthy of a spot in Beach Home Monthly or something. I laughed at the absurdity. My best friend Beth would like it though. I snapped a couple pictures and sent them along with a few before photos. The difference was shocking.

"Lily, it looks great." Her voice blared from the phone as I set it on the dresser while I wrapped up the roller and tapped the lid back onto the paint can.

"I really like it. I did the same colour scheme in the master bedroom, but I haven't yet moved everything back into place."

"Decided to go with my palette, eh?"

"Why not? You're the best in the biz."

Beth was a highly sought-after interior design expert. She'd been lucky enough to have been a featured designer on a couple of home renovation shows. After those aired, she booked months, if not years, in advance.

"I was analyzing the living room photos, and I really think you should paint the bookcases sea grey. It won't stand out like a sore thumb, but it'll look nice. I think if you put a nice panoramic above, but in a white frame, it'll just add that something you need. Do you have a pano? You know what, never mind. I'll send you some ideas."

"Keep them reasonable in cost."

"They're from staging's."

From magazine shoots. The pictures typically stored in a warehouse, hung for a few photo shoots in local magazines and taken back. Beth got access to their inventory on the cheap and had a long list of things she could sell to her friends, myself included.

"Don't go crazy."

"Me?" She laughed. "Never."

I slumped on the bed and admired my handiwork. Sure, it was only fresh paint on the walls, but it was amazing how much it changed the feel in the room. It no longer was the place I'd played with my Barbies, or the room I'd sneak out of when my parents started snoring. Now it had a grownup sense, sophisticated even, ready for a new beginning.

For guests.

For a possible new family in the fall.

"You can bring them out when you come for a visit."

Beth scoffed. "Or you can come and pick them up when you come to your senses."

And here we go again. "I know you and Dina and Amelia all think I lost my mind."

"You did. You ran away. Take your little pity break, clear your mind and come home where you belong." If I didn't know better, it sounded like she just gave me a scolding, complete with a nagging whine.

"As I told you before I left, I'm staying the summer." I flaked off a piece of dried paint from my finger.

"I know that's what you said, but you'll change your mind. Lily, I know you. You need all the modern conveniences you're not going to find in your small hippie town. You hated that place, remember?"

"It's not a hippie little town." And I only hated it after the incident.

"Really?" Even over the phone, I heard her eyebrow rise.

"Fine. It's hippie-like, but the beach is so relaxing." I'd been here for a few days, and even though I was working hard painting and moving furniture, it had been oddly relaxing. The ocean scent, the salt in the breeze. Soon

I was going to be splashing in the ocean.

"That's my point. You'll get some peace for a bit, relax and unwind, and then you'll tuck your tail between your legs, come home and face the music. You're not thinking of having the baby there, are you? Oh god, Lily, please tell me you're going to come home to modern medicine and have the baby in the hospital?" Desperation, mixed with a heavily pleading tone, oozed from her voice making her sound more like my mother than my best friend.

It hadn't been something I'd completely worked out, but I supposed it was something else to add to my checklist. The nearest major hospital was an hour away, but there were clinics and outpatient facilities within an easy drive, and they were all modern. I still lived in a first world country, and I was having a baby, not major surgery, but still. I should be under someone's care. At least that was a point I was going to take.

"Oh, Lily, you're stalling. Please tell me you're going to come home to have the baby."

I shrugged. "It's likely, okay?"

Her relief washed over the phone. "Oh, thank god. You haven't gone bat-shit crazy."

"I'm not crazy at all."

"Completely, especially for going back there. After everything that happened. I still can't believe *that's* where you chose to run to. You wouldn't catch me returning."

My heart took a little beating. "You're not going to come for a visit? I just painted your room."

"You're not going to be there long enough for me to need to come. I give it another two weeks. Tops. You'll be home before then."

"It's going to take me more than a couple of weeks to ready this place." Sure, it was possible to list as it was, but I'd never get market price for it. However, put a little TLC into it, and modernise it, and well, I likely wouldn't need to worry about cashflow in the short future.

Another voice whispered in the background.

"Just a sec." A deep sigh breathed over the line. "Thank you, Courtney." Her admin assistant. Once again, Beth's voice became clearer. "Hey, Lil? Why is Parker calling me?"

My mouth went dry as cotton and if I hadn't already been sitting, surely I would've collapsed on the bed. "I honestly don't have the faintest idea. He's called me a few times."

"So, you've talked to him?"

"Why would I give him the time of day? He left me, remember?"

"Yeah, and I'll never forgive him for that. But he can't call my office, that's unacceptable. We both know that shithead isn't looking for an interior designer. He's looking for you."

Which was true. Parker had all the decorating sense of a seventeen-year-old comic boy. Swords and movie paraphernalia didn't belong in the living room, and no matter how I tried to encourage him, he didn't want to change. Good thing we did all the entertaining at my apartment.

"Deal with him before I have to."

It wouldn't end well for Parker if Beth got to speak her mind. Since the moment we had started dating, she's had her back up to him and they never got along. When he walked out on me, she was ready to tear him a new one, and if he kept calling her office, he'd likely to get it.

"I'll think about it."

"Aren't you the least bit curious why he's calling?" The inflection in her voice told me she was.

"Not at all." Although I was, however, it was more fear-based curiosity than anything else.

Beth cleared her throat. "Look, I have a meeting with a client in a minute. I got to go. Call me soon."

"Love you."

"You too." And with that, the line went dead.

Chapter Four

resh and paint-free, I knocked on Eric's door. Checking my reflection on the screen door, I gave my hair another smoothing and inhaled sharply.

"Come in, it's unlocked."

With trepidation, I stepped inside, balancing the apple pie I'd picked up on a whim. Eric's floorplan was smaller than mine, but we both had our kitchens at the back of the house, looking out towards the setting sun and the Pacific Ocean. The colour on his walls was a bright blue, but it worked well with the washed-out table and chairs.

"Please, make yourself at home."

"Thanks. For you." I handed him the box.

"Ooh, Sylvia's Bakery. This is really nice." The grin on his face was hard to look away from.

I took the water bottle he offered, our fingertips touching just enough to feel the electricity as I let my gaze linger over his fine form. Even though I wasn't ready for anything in that department, it never hurt to check out anyone. He really had grown and filled out. Who knew the gangly little boy would turn into such a handsome guy? And a sweet one at that?

"I'd give you a beer, but…" His eyes fell to my tummy.

"This works." I wandered through his living room, staring at all the pictures hanging on the walls and those set on neatly stacked bookshelves. "How's your family doing?" There was a tri-fold frame with a younger version of Eric on one side, his older brother on the other and a sweet pic of his parents in the middle. Based on the ages of the boys, and that teenage awkwardness, I pegged the pictures to be at least fifteen years old.

God, we had it good, and we didn't even know it. Life was so much easier back then.

"Mom's good. Living the high life in Arizona with my step-dad."

I searched his face when I heard the hurt in his voice and walked back over to the kitchen. "Awe. I had no idea they split." Mind you, I really hadn't been keeping up with what was going on around these parts.

"They didn't." His face fell. "Dad died six years ago."

I rested my weary butt on one of the stools around

his bar-height table. "Geez, that sucks. I'm sorry for your loss. Were you close?"

A weathered expression filled his face and dulled the shine in his eyes. "Yeah."

"Aww, I'm really sorry. That's rough."

"Yep, so I know what you're going through. It's not easy." He passed me an empty plate. "Sorry, it's nothing fancy, just pulled pork sandwiches and salad. And I only threw in the salad because I figured you needed your nutrients."

It was cute, and a small smile leaked out unsuspecting from my lips. "That's very nice. And this looks delicious." Following Eric's movements, I opened a huge hamburger bun and piled on the sweet-smelling pork onto one half. Closing it up, I scooped out some runny coleslaw onto my plate.

"You good if we eat out on the deck?"

"Sounds delightful." Where my deck was completely open aired, Eric's had been screened, so it allowed all the fresh air minus the little flying pests that always seemed to come out when there was food around. I sat in one of the Adirondack chairs and took a bite of my sandwich. It was heavenly. "This is really good."

"I'll take it as a high compliment."

There was an under current of a tone, but I couldn't quite put my finger on what it was.

"So, since I dropped all my drama on your lap, why don't you tell me your story." I took another bite.

"I have no story."

I found that hard to believe. Everyone had a story. Everyone had a past. I swallowed down my bite before speaking. "I don't buy it."

"Why not?" He faced me and took a long pull from his bottle.

I shrugged. "Because I can't believe that you... Well..." Whatever was going to follow that, likely was going to come across as rude, so I closed my mouth. "What made you come back and live here permanently? You were a city dweller in summers past."

"Got tired of the hustle and bustle, and a life that was always go-go-go."

I was a city girl, born and raised, who only came to the beach in the summer. Go-go-go was just how life was. "The city, especially in the winter, has so much to offer. There's always the theatre and museums and an endless array of activities to keep a person busy."

"Why does one have to be busy constantly to be fulfilled?"

"Because they do." It's just what adults did - worked all the time, made a decent living, enjoyed life when they could.

"You mean to tell me you can't just sit here for

hours staring out into that?" He pointed out to the endless horizon.

Yes, the view was spectacular and soothing, but no, I couldn't spend hours just staring. I'd need something to do – read a book at the bare minimum, but I was more likely to paint or work and glance at it occasionally. As it was, I hadn't truly rested since I arrived. There was just always something that required my attention. I hadn't even had a swim in the Pacific Ocean. "Nope. Not possible. For me, anyway."

"That's why I'm not a guy who's big on that kind of life. There was nothing beyond here that begged me to leave this all behind. After a day's work, I can sit here and just enjoy the beauty of nature."

The Darth Vader theme marched right into the conversation. *Damn you, Parker. As always, your timing stinks.*

I dug out my phone and flipped the switch to silent. He could call all night if he wanted, I wasn't answering. See how he liked it. Jerk.

"That same caller." If there was a tsk on the tip of his tongue, it was gone in a flash.

I sighed and took a sip of my water. "It's my ex."

Eric faced me, his gaze landing on the phone. "The baby daddy?"

A slow bob followed. "Yeah."

"Does he know you're here?"

"The only person who knows the actual location is Beth, my best friend. My other besties know I'm at my summer home, but they don't know where that is."

"And this ex?" Was worry woven into his words?

"He doesn't know the location either. It was never brought up."

It was best if Parker didn't know that part of my life, so it never came up in conversation. In the brief time we dated, we never visited my summer home and the words Cheshire Bay never left my lips. There weren't even memories of it hanging in the apartment. As far as Parker knew, my life began at twenty when I finally went to college.

"He knows about the baby, right?"

"Oh yeah. Cleared out his drawer the next day and left."

Eric laughed, a sweet, gentle sound that matched the roll of the ocean waves. "His drawer?"

"For when he spent the night. Still had his place, just mine was nicer. Not quite a shrine to the Marvel and DC Comics and Lord of the Rings art deco."

"You were dating a nerd?" His laugh grew in strength.

"Why is that funny?"

He wiped the smile off with a cupping of his hand.

"Well, when you were here last, you were, well…"

I hung my head in shame. "Yeah. I was into the bad boys, I know."

"The badder, the better." The words slipped out so easily.

I flipped my gaze back to the ocean, a river of hurt coursing through my veins. "That was a long time ago."

"I know."

My resolve faltered, but my tone was clipped. "People change."

"I know that too."

His plate rocked on the tiny table when he set it down, but I didn't turn his way. I wanted to get up and storm away but figured that was more in line with the way I was. As a grown adult, I liked to face my problems head on and deal with things. Except for the vibrating phone under my palm. Damn Parker. I needed to prepare for that battle.

Eric cleared his throat. "I'm sorry."

"You have nothing to apologise for."

He shuffled in his chair and his foot scuffed over the floor. "I do. I invited you over for dinner and now I've made you uncomfortable. I'm a terrible host."

"If you can accept that my past is in my past and I can't do anything about it, we'll be just fine." I needed one friend here while I holed up and hid, tail tucked between my legs, as Beth would say.

"I guess I was jealous, and that jealousy reared up."

"Jealous?" I twisted to face him and arched an eyebrow. "What were you jealous of?"

"Your life. Your outlook. My parents were so strict, I didn't attend many beach parties. And you, you were the life of every party. I wanted a girl like you, but girls like you don't date nerds."

Which was entirely true. Sad but true. "I'm sorry I treated unfairly." I scrapped a fingernail under the wrapping on my water bottle.

"You were never mean or anything. At least not to me or London."

A smidgen, a very small sprinkle of it, settled over me.

Eric patted my arm. "Don't worry about it. Like you said, people change and we're adults now."

"Yes, we are. Complete with adult responsibilities and all the stuff our parents warned us about." That made him giggle, and I was happy to hear it. It meant the evening wasn't a total bust. "Tell me about your job. Being a pilot must be so interesting."

The grandest smile stretched from ear to ear. "There was a fundraiser going on a few years back, and they had a win a flight around the island. I entered and won. I was so excited, I talked non-stop, and the pilot suggested

I look into lessons, and one thing led to another. So… I worked my butt off on the docks to save up money for flight school. It's a better way to travel." A peaceful glow filled his face. "Up in the sky, that's my happy place."

"That's awesome. It really is. Good for you doing what you love."

"What about you?"

"I'm still working on figuring that part out." I thought I'd found it with Parker, oddly enough. But with the distance between us, I knew he wasn't the one. I was better off without him, even if I had extra responsibilities because of it.

"Let me know if I can help." He sat there in silence for a few heartbeats while my phone continued its incessant vibrations. Didn't Parker have anything better to do? Leave a message for crying out loud. "I'm going to grab another beer. Want anything else to drink?"

"I'm good." I rose, picked up our plates and helped clean the kitchen. "Thanks for dinner. I really appreciated it."

It was nice to have someone else decide what to eat, and I didn't have to try and figure out what to create that didn't come out of a cooler while I waited for a new fridge to arrive. Sandwiches were starting to bore me as I couldn't make them as well as the deli around the corner from my apartment did. Damn, they were tasty, and I could eat a mean BLT right about now.

"Anytime. It's nice to have someone to eat with."

"I agree." I caught a shy smile forming on his lips, but it disappeared before I could capture it to memory.

Eric walked me to the door and tipped his head toward the pile of wood stacked by the entrance. "What's with the plywood sheets?"

"I need to refloor the upstairs deck."

"I never pegged you for a handyman, or handywoman."

I placed my hand on my hip and pouted the cutest way I knew how. "It can't be that hard. Pull up the old boards, nail in the new ones. Stain. Lay out a carpet and voila."

He laughed. "Okay, Bob Villa. That sounds about right." There was something charming about the way he said it. "Call me if you need an extra set of hands."

"I'll hold you to it, even if just to laugh as I make an ass out of myself."

"Sounds like a plan."

And a plan with Eric and his easy going way was something I could get behind.

Chapter Five

eth texted me a picture of a lovely panoramic for the living room that I *just had to have*, and I lifted my phone above the bookcase I was currently painting in the light of day. She had a gift, as from the tiny image, it appeared to match perfectly with the colour schemes. I approved her choice and without much else said, she mentioned it would be sent ASAP. She was also going to bring out some other staging materials and prep for a quick photo op, but only stay for one night.

I rolled my eyes since she hadn't given me a date at all, but at least it would be a visit. I missed my friend.

I went back to painting the top inside of the bookcase when a knock sounded on my door. "Just a second," I hollered back, hopped down off the stepladder and turned down the music. "Yes?"

A strange man from the hardware store stood at my

door. "Lily Davies?" He read my name off the clipboard and ran his gaze up and down my body. After I stopped visiting Cheshire Bay, I changed my name to my mother's maiden name.

"Yes."

He tipped his head to the side and stared at me hard, a look of recognition blooming as it clicked. "Wait a sec, you're Lily Baker. Miss Long Beach 2003. I used to have the calendar. Oh my god. The guys will go wild when they find out."

Not one of my finest moments, but I refused to go there. At least the calendar raised money for a local charity, so it wasn't a complete joke.

"Can I help you?"

"It's me, Josh."

The name didn't ring a bell. At all. Even as I tried remembering if I'd ever seen his face before. The kid looked a few years younger than me.

"Josh Mulaney?" His voiced cracked with excitement. "I worked at Scoops."

"Oh, hi." The name, swirling with weak memories of him and his buddies around a campfire smoking weed floated into my brain, as did the other, more unpleasant ones. The dancing. The kissing. The sex. I shuddered.

His eyes settled on my bump, and suddenly he was all business, which admittedly, was perfectly okay by me.

"I'm here to deliver your fridge and haul the old one away."

"Finally. Wasn't that supposed to arrive yesterday?"

Island time was a whole different ballgame, but still. I had been expecting this to arrive at least twenty-four hours ago.

I stepped aside. "I've cleared a path."

Now it was time to make myself scarce, and I grabbed an apple to munch on the deck while Josh did his work.

When all was said and done, he passed me the work order *and* his card. "If you'd like to join our Canada Day Bash, my number is on the back. The guys and I are always up for a good time." The wink he gave me made me uncomfortable, and I took a step back.

I waved the card. "Well, thank you."

He tipped his hat and headed back outside.

I closed and locked the door, gagging at the thought of being thirty and slutty. My past was in the past. Who I was at fifteen and sixteen was a far cry from who I am now. Maybe coming to the beach house was a bad idea.

Hours later, after verifying my new fridge was cooling properly, I went to the grocery store just off the strip and selected a wide variety of perishables and dairy products, while simultaneously trying to ignore the whispers, most of which came from people I didn't recognise. Why hadn't I physically changed as much as everyone else had? At the bare minimum, I should've dyed my hair to a dark brown instead of leaving it the sun-kissed blonde it had always been.

Every aisle, there was another snide remark.

I told you she was back.

Wonder what's she doing here, thought we made it clear she wasn't welcome.

Tramp.

Look at her, all knocked up. Getting what she deserves. Heard her husband left her. What trash.

I ignored them or at least didn't give them any indication I'd been privy to their comments, even if some of it was inaccurate. He was my ex-boyfriend, not my ex-husband, but in the grand scheme of things, I was still on my own.

I set my groceries by the cashier, who looked at me as if I'd just sprouted two horns and spit all over my items.

"Thought it was you." There was so much vitriol in her voice. Her nametag read Kim, and all I pictured was Jordan's older sister, but the ages didn't seem to match up. That Kim was my age, a goodie-two-shoes like Mona, but the person before me seemed at least ten years older.

I continued to stack my items on one end and raced

45

to the other side to bag them, since she was piling them up. Rather than make a scene, I loaded the three bags back into my cart and handed her my credit card.

"No credit. Cash only." She rolled her eyes and turned her nose up like a putrid smell rolled off me.

Since when? I checked the sign hanging above to verify I hadn't stepped into a cash only line. I hadn't. "I don't have that much cash."

"Then put something back."

A line formed behind me.

"Are you sure you won't accept the credit card?" I lifted it again to show her.

"I said *cash only*." She crossed her arms over her ample chest.

I dug through my purse, coming up with about half of what I needed.

The guy in line directly behind me sighed.

I apologised profusely and started pulling items out of my bag, things I didn't need tonight at least. I'd come back later for them. One by one, Kim slowly deducted them off the bill, giving me a total I had the right cash for. I handed her the bills. She took each and ran a blacklight over them.

"Checking for counterfeit."

For crying out loud. I wanted to scream, but instead, I bit my tongue to the point where I drew blood.

She dropped the change into my hand, which I barely caught, and tossed my receipt. Even if I wanted to explain I wasn't responsible for Jordan's death, as his death had been ruled non-criminal and an accident, I held back. Swallowing the pity I had for her as she clearly wasn't going to let it go, I simply picked up the paper and tucked it into my bag. I wasn't ten feet away when the guy behind me spoke.

"Who the hell was that?"

"Lily Baker."

"She's back?"

"Bitch can go to hell."

I froze for a heartbeat but kept walking out to my jeep. It wasn't until I pulled in front of my house that I allowed the dam to break, and the tears to flood. A part of me wanted to call the manager and voice a complaint, but I wasn't sure what that would accomplish, except put another target on my back. I rested my head against the steering wheel, giving into the feelings. As I reached for a tissue, I spotted Eric waving.

I sent a half-hearted wave back in his direction.

He pointed and gestured via sign language asking if I was okay.

Wiping my eyes, I hopped out. "Sorry, just having a girl moment. Pregnancy hormones and all."

His brows pinched together, and he walked over.

"Really? That's some hormones."

A glance at my reflection was enough to confirm and agree. My eyes were puffy and red. I was not one of those girls who cried pretty. Every cry turned me into an ugly disaster, and the raccoon eyes didn't help. I ran my fingers under my eyes and wiped away the moisture and blackness. Walking to the back of the Jeep, I lifted the end gate and grabbed a bag. "I'm fine, honestly."

"Where'd you go shopping?" He handled one of the reusable bags with a logo from a small Italian bakery four blocks from my apartment.

"Houseman's."

The name must've been explanation enough as he dropped his questions and brought the bags in behind me. I stopped and stared at the kind gesture, I hadn't expected him to follow.

"Sorry. I maybe should've asked if you needed a hand."

"It's nice of you to help out." I put the bags on the counter and started unloading. "When did they switch to a cash only system?"

Eric was checking out my paint job, but he stopped and spun around. "What? No one ever uses cash."

I slammed the fridge after putting in a jug of milk, rattling a stack of Mom's favourite dishes. I hadn't thrown everything away. "For real?"

He stepped back. "Yeah. Who told you that?"

I shook my head, regretting my desire to get out of Houseman's rather than speak to a manager. "It doesn't matter." Next time, I'd go in armed with more cash just to have her think she'd caught me off guard. Even if it was more than that.

Eric handed me a bag of lettuce. "I'm going to have a few people over tonight and have a fire out on the beach. You're welcome to come join me. Us, I mean." The invite lingered in the air.

A fire would be great, and I certainly enjoyed Eric's company, but there would be others, and after today... "I don't know." I searched his face for answers.

"If it helps, they're friends of mine. You may or may not remember them."

"Will they remember me?" It was a terrible thing to ask because it sounded like I was self-centered.

Fifteen years ago, I was a horribly shallow bitch, but no one seemed to understand how that was a long time ago, and sometimes stupid people did selfish things and yet grow up to be decent adults.

"Maybe. I never asked." He shrugged and passed me a bag of bagels. "Sylvia's has much nicer, and larger, bagels."

"I know, I just forgot." I stared out my kitchen window, right into the side of Eric's but I couldn't bare to look at him.

"You okay?"

"Yeah. I'm just peachy." I hung my head for a moment to catch my breath and ground myself. Shaking off the pity party building, I turned slowly and inhaled to a count of five. "What do you think of the paint job? Do you think the colour works?"

His gaze raked me in, but he refocused on the freshly painted wall. "Looks great. This the same colour you used upstairs?"

"All inside walls have this smoke colour, yep."

"I like it." He stepped around a pile of books and a table full of old knickknacks, nearly falling into the sofa to avoid it all. "What are you doing with this stuff?"

"Don't know. I'll probably pack up most of it since it doesn't mean anything to me. I tend to be a minimalist and clutter hurts my soul on a level most wouldn't understand."

He laughed. "Don't take too long a look at my place then."

It hadn't been that bad when I was there. Sure, it was a little cluttered, but it wasn't overwhelming. Not like how I felt looking at my own living room in its current condition. "I assure you, it was fine."

A buzzer sounded from the back of his jean pocket. "Oops. I gotta run. I have a charter flight leaving in an hour for Seattle. I'll be back for the bonfire tonight. While I'm gone, consider joining us?" His offer was so sweet, as was the gentle pleading tone he used. "We're a tame bunch – too old to truly party it up."

That alone tipped the scales in his favour, but I wasn't about to give in yet. "I'll think about it."

"It's a start." He gave me a little wave and the screen door banged as he left.

Chapter Six

y time the sun set, I had four boxes packed tightly with useless books and trinkets, and my bookcases were rearranged in an acceptable order, with the correct ratio of stacked books to knickknacks. I stood back and admired the handiwork, taking a picture to send to Beth. With the blinds pulled down, and the ambient lighting in the living room, the area had a soft yet useable appeal to it. A place I could curl up with a book and watch the rolling ocean or entertain a couple of friendly people, should it be raining. Yep, as a whole, I was happy with the way the living room looked. It was starting to feel like a home, and not a vacation home.

Footsteps jumped up onto my back deck and a knuckle cracked against the frame.

An image of Parker had suddenly appeared, but I blinked it away and focused. "Eric." My hand fell to my chest as a bolt of adrenaline coursed through my body.

"Did you give any more thought to coming out? We just got the fire going." Long gone was the dress shirt and khakis from earlier and in its place, he wore shorts and a V-neck tee. Saturday night bonfire attire. Perfect.

"Is it that time already?" Truly, I'd lost track of it while reorganizing items that no longer had much relevance, even Mona wouldn't want them, and she kept just about everything. "You know, I haven't even eaten yet."

"Perfect. There's hotdogs and marshmallows."

Ew. Marshmallows were gross, but the idea of having a hotdog sounded fantastic. I hadn't had one in years. I weighed the option of staying inside and avoiding the desire to look outside and spy on my grown-up neighbour, or just sucking up what will be and getting it over with. Eric's friends were bound to know who I was, and if they didn't, they would soon enough. Rumours circulated and whispers followed.

My warring debate would've gone on longer if not for the sweet smile plastered on Eric's chiselled face, and the light lean on my door frame that suggested he could outwait me or find another endearing way of asking. I didn't deserve the olive branch he was constantly offering, based on the past, but I was thrilled he hadn't given up. It warmed my heart knowing I had a friend here.

"Fine. Let me grab a sweater."

He waited, and after flipping all lights off but the under the cabinet ones, we descended over to the bonfire well under way.

"Hey, everyone, this is my neighbour, Lily."

I held my breath as I scanned the faces one by one. Either they truly didn't know who I was, or they didn't care. A wave of relief washed over me, and I stood beside an empty chair a guy opened as I approached.

"Go ahead," Eric said, pointing to the space, as he introduced his buddies.

"This is Mitch and his girlfriend Cedar." He walked behind them and squeezed their shoulders. "Cedar works at the check-in gate at the airport and has amazing knowledge about the area, so just ask if you need something. Mitch is the mechanic who services my plane. He's also the baggage handler and all-around minion who just happens to be my best friend." A loving expression warmed his face.

I glanced up to Eric. "You have your own plane?" How cool was that?

Even with the glow from the flames, a new colour tinged his cheeks. "Don't get too excited. It's only a six-seater, twin-prop Cessna. And an older model to boot. That's why I need a great mechanic like Mitch here."

"Still, that's pretty nifty."

Cedar laughed and tugged on one of her side braids. "Nifty. I like that word. It should be used more often." Her smile was infectious.

"This is Jesse, the local mortician." Eric stepped another spot over to the lone gentleman. "He moved here a few years back and lives two doors away from me, three from you." He pointed down the beach.

"Oh, that way." I laughed, only because I was the last house at the end of the lane.

It made Eric grin too. "Yeah." He winked. "Is Jenna coming?" He asked Jesse.

"Nah. She's not feeling well." But he didn't make eye contact and grabbed for a hot dog stick.

"Next time."

"Maybe." He squirmed in his chair and positioned the stick over the fire.

Eric moved around the growing bonfire to the other couple, the last of the group. "And this is Willow and her husband Arlo."

"Do you work at the airport too?" I asked since Eric hadn't volunteered any information.

"Not at all." Willow spoke up. "Arlo owns the bait and tackle shop on the wharf, and I'm a midwife."

Eric chuckled. "See, I told you it would be good for you to come." He moved a camping chair closer to me.

"A midwife?" I didn't know what that was and

55

looked around hoping someone would fill me in.

"I help women birth their babies."

"Oh, like an obstetrician." Which reminded me again to locate one, as I was close to needing a check up.

She crossed her legs and leaned forward. "Similar, but I help them birth in their homes. Birth doesn't have to be a medical event, it's a very natural part of life."

"I agree."

However, the idea of a homebirth didn't appeal at all. It had to be messy, and all the new mother needed was to clean up after just given birth. No wonder I'd never heard of her profession. It didn't sound ideal at all.

"And she gives extensive prenatal care too," her husband piped up, the pride oozing through is words. "None of those thirty second appointments like you'd get with a doctor. Willow's appointments take thirty minutes at least."

I stared at her, trying to hide my curiosity. "How long does it take to stick a finger up my insides and tell me to come back in a month?" Because that was all my doctor back home did. Oh, and he added everything was textbook. Didn't need a thirty-minute appointment for that.

She chuckled, a sweet melodic sound. "Oh, we don't even do an internal exam unless we think its necessary. Mostly we talk. Discuss the emotional aspects, the physical changes, and go over any questions you have.

It's really a no pressure visit."

"It sounds… well…" Definitely different. "Like it's something to consider while I'm here."

It wasn't something I was going to explore right here on the beach, but if I couldn't find an OB in the area, I'd consider giving her a call. Poor Beth would roll her eyes at the idea of me giving birth in my living room, if it ever got to that, which was highly unlikely since I'd planned on being back home before that became reality.

"Hungry?" Eric passed me a raw hotdog already stabbed onto a stick.

I took it, my fingers grazing his as I did and looked deep into his eyes. "Starving."

Time hadn't erased the ability to properly cook a hotdog over an open flame, and when it was cooked to perfection, I wrapped a bun around it and slid it off.

A container of condiments came my way, and I shook my head. Instead, I took a hearty bite. And it was so good. A river of grease escaped my lips, and Eric pointed it to and hesitated as if he wanted to wipe it himself. Instead, I reached for a napkin and dabbed it myself while I continued to gaze upon him as the bonfire cast flickers of light and shadows across his face.

Silently, he passed me a can of coke, his fingers touching mine longer than need be, although I wasn't going to complain.

* * *

Sitting around the fire had been everything I hadn't known I needed. I wasn't aware how much I longed for the connection that came from deep belly laughter and great company until I was snorting from an off-colour joke Mitch told, and playfully grabbing Eric's arm as I tried to catch my breath.

When the stars started twinkling, Arlo brought out his guitar and plucked out a few songs for us. We didn't sing along, but it was peaceful listening to his fingers strum. Clearly, the way he played, he wasn't a beginner, and I knew most of the traditional songs he hummed along to, but the folksier ones were new.

The time ticked on as the full moon cast shadows along the beach, and the fire died down to glowing embers. It was well past midnight, and time to bid adieu to the small beach party.

"Time to call it a night," Willow declared and folded her and Arlo's chairs. "It was lovely meeting you." Her hug reminded me of the kind you'd give an old friend, long and lingering with a touch of comfort. I didn't want to let go.

"Stay safe and peace out," Arlo said, packing up his guitar. He wrapped a hand around his wife's waist, and the two of them disappeared between our homes.

Mitch collapsed his chair and helped a tipsy Cedar out of hers. All the way to their car, her giggle echoed off the houses, and only when it was silent, did I suspect she was tucked into Mitch's vehicle.

Jesse said goodnight, and shuffled down the beach to his place, which was indeed, only two down from Eric's.

I assisted Eric in putting out the fire, making sure the coals were extinguished. The cool ocean waves lapped at my feet as I scooped up a bucket of water and a deep sizzling sound escaped the fire when I poured it over top. In the light of the moon, smoke trails shot towards the heavens.

"Thanks for inviting me tonight." I walked beside Eric up to the dry sand stretching across the ocean-facing part of our homes.

"I'm so glad."

"It was nice to not be reminded of who I was." And for a few hours, to not even have thought about it.

"They're good people and they were once crazy teenagers too. We all were, and we all grew up."

"Did they all live here too?"

We all seemed to be about the same age, but I didn't recognize them. Truly, my teenage years were a wasteland of selfishness and ignorance.

"Willow and Arlo were born and raised here, and Mitch is from the other side, near Nanaimo. Cedar grew up on a commune in the northern part of the island."

Of course, they were all islanders.

I was the odd one out. The city girl.

"You did fine, Lily." Eric stopped walking and stared at me. "Stop worrying so much."

"I wasn't worrying." *Much.* He stood so close, but I wasn't frightened. At least not in a bad way. I was worried Eric had read too much into my playfulness, as the moonlight bathed his face in a soft glow, and there was a twinkle in his eye.

At least my instincts weren't wrong, and Eric leaned his face in, but I put my hand on his chest to stop him.

"I can't." I lowered my head and took a step back, even though the rush of imagining his lips on mine was strong. "I'm sorry." I rubbed my tummy as a reminder.

There would be no romance, there couldn't even be what I was known for best back in the day - a quick romp in the hay.

"That's fine."

Waves rolled against the beach and washed back out to sea, and in the distance an owl hooted.

Eric cast his gaze down and kicked at the sand. "I understand."

"Thank you." I inhaled sharply, not wanting to leave him.

The timing was all wrong for anything to develop between us. A few months back, maybe? I took another step up into my place, my hand slowly trialing on the banister, a deep longing building in my gut. It didn't matter how Eric had showed more compassion towards me in my short time here than anyone else… It couldn't work.

My mouth hung open; there was much I wanted to explain, and more I should apologize for, but the words failed to come out of my lips. "Goodnight."

A sadness filled my soul and the deep longing throbbed without release.

Eric deserved better than the likes of me. He deserved someone who hadn't run afoul of the law.

Chapter Seven

week after the beach party, aside from the upper deck, I had transformed my house into something I could live in, and a place I truly loved. Long gone were the ancient pictures and tacky fillers. I'd filled the back of my Jeep up three times with items and hauled them off to the reuse center in Spirit Bay. Thanks to the internet, I'd even ordered couch covers, and for a fraction of the cost of replacing the furniture, I was able to update them with a whole new look.

I placed a tarp out on the sand and pinned it into place, and mentally prepped myself for extracting the kitchen table from the house and out onto my temporary workspace. I had it all planned out, and knew exactly how to wiggle it out, without removing the table legs as I was trying to save myself some time. Plus, I checked how they were attached, and some sort of super glue must've been used. There were only the flat tops of a nail head visible, and not a nice screw head like the one in my apartment had.

I dragged the table out, but it caught on something inside, likely the end of the counter. I tried to push it back in but could only move it so far. The table weighed more than I did, and it was difficult at best. Despite my best grunts and snorts, the damn thing seemed to be firmly lodged in the door.

"Son-of-a-bitch."

"Everything okay over there?" Eric's voice was sleepy yet rugged.

"Just fine." I shook it with all my strength, which wasn't much anymore. With a heavy sigh, I stepped back and wiped the sweat off my brow. What the hell was I going to do now?

Eric came out onto his back deck in his pajamas; a white top and checkered bottoms. His hair was matted down on one side in a charming and endearing manner. He walked to the edge of his deck and looked over into mine. "Did you get it stuck?"

My focus returned to the now permanent door stop. "Nope. Just needed a break from taking it outside." A laugh tainted my words, but a minor ache stretched across my lower belly, and I instinctively cradled my belly.

In a heartbeat, he stood on my porch barefooted, and stared at my expanding waistline. His smile dropped to the floor. "Everything okay?"

The pain subsided. "Just fine." I replaced the grimace with a smile.

Thankfully, once I gave the table an attempted shake, his grin reappeared.

"Ah, you got it wedged in there good and tight, I see." He stretched, and I stole a peek at the tight abs as his shirt lifted a teasing amount.

"Not wedged, just…" I caved and tossed my hands up in defeat. "Fine, it's stuck."

"Take the legs off."

"No can do. They are nailed on."

"Seriously? Handmade table?" He bent over to admire the handiwork. "Wow. That's a beaute."

"Think my dad made it." But I really had no idea. It had always been in the house as far back as I could remember.

Eric climbed up and over and stood in my kitchen. "I think you should've gone the other way."

"I had it all worked out on paper. It should've been a smooth move." I pointed to the grid paper and cut out I'd created.

"That's seriously detailed." Eric picked up the paper and moved the cut out around. "But you forgot a tiny detail." He flipped the moveable piece onto its side and demonstrated.

"Well, damn." Of course, now I saw the errors of my way.

"You refinishing this?"

"Yes." I narrowed my eyes. What was he thinking?

"Might need to refinish the frame too." He ran his hand over the dark-brown doorframe.

I stared at it. If we pushed hard enough to scratch the tabletop, the door frame was also going to get a solid scuffing.

"Can you lift on your side?"

I tried but the whole thing was jammed. "Not an inch."

Eric climbed over to where I stood and gave it a lift. "It's moving."

"Look at you go, He-Man."

"That's all I need for now," he grunted and shimmied the table enough to unwedge it. "Can you get back over to the other side?"

I was neither cute nor sexy as I crawled under the table legs, and before I made it to the other end, I froze. Written in marker, near the corner leg, was a brief note. *For Madeline. Love Marcus.* The date was over thirty years ago, around the time my big sister was born.

My heart fluttered at the gesture. Dad sure loved Mom, and everyone knew it.

I heaved myself to a standing position and together

we pushed it back into the kitchen, tipped it on its side, and twisted it around to manoeuvre it through the doorway much easier. We set it on the tarp, and I ran my hand over the tabletop. Hardly any digs and dents, and the scratches were surface enough to come off with a quick sanding.

"Thank you." I gave my belly a solid rub to soothe the ache but tried passing it off as stretching.

It failed as Eric continued to stare at the bump, although he refrained from speaking the question dancing in his eyes.

Instead, he ran his hands through his hair, smoothing down the stuck-up part. "We're a good team."

The words lingered in the ocean fresh air.

Can't happen. "Can I make you a coffee?" A distraction, that's what I needed. It was too early in the day to think of dreams and other worldly possibilities. Those were other people's futures, not mine. There was no team in single motherhood.

"Can I brush my teeth first?"

I nodded. "Of course."

He dashed off, and once out of sight I prepped a quick caffeine and sugar rush kick. The cup was ready when he darkened my doorstep.

"Help yourself to milk in the fridge. The sugar is on the counter. Oh, and the chocolate chip muffins are good too."

"I like it black, thanks, but I'll grab a muffin."

I grabbed my full mug and went out to sit on the patio with Eric hot on my heels. We made idle chitchat about the upcoming change in the weather and where I managed to find a sander, until I put my mug down. It was time to address the tiny elephant in the room.

"So, Eric." Verbal diarrhea was my strong point, and I really needed to watch how I phrased my words. Last thing I wanted to do was alienate the guy since he'd proven to be a sweet man and a great neighbour. "About last week, at the bonfire."

"Don't worry about it. It was all my fault." But he wouldn't look me in the eye, much like he'd avoided me over the past seven days. Aside from a neighbourly wave here and there, the conversations had been minimal, reduced to a hello or have a great day.

"But it's not. Maybe I led you to believe…"

"You did no such thing. I have a bad habit of reading too much into situations."

I twisted my body toward him, and I gave my belly a light rub. The ache was still there, but it wasn't screaming mad. Perhaps I overdid it. "How so?" Maybe he'd spill about past girlfriends.

"It doesn't matter." He swirled his mug on the edge of his chair and pulled deeper into himself.

"What did she do?"

"What makes you think it was a *she* that did something?"

"Because you're not with someone. Like I said before, everyone has a story."

"Yeah? Well, not me." There was such a finality to his tone that I backed off. He stared out into the ocean; the crests bigger than they had been since I arrived - a storm was brewing out on the sea. "Might be a good day to go surfing."

How I wish. That would require me to be able to get into my bikini, not that I think it would fit anymore, and no one really needed to see my huge baby bump in the raw, stretchmarks and all. Plus, my balance wasn't what it used to be.

"Think I'll stick to sanding the table and all that jazz. After that, just the upstairs deck remains as part of my grand overhaul to the house plans go."

"It's looking very nice."

"Thank you."

Lately, the idea of selling the beach house had popped up in my mind, growing in strength with each passing day. It didn't help that everywhere I went, people stopped their regular conversations to stare and whisper behind my back. If it was here and there, it wouldn't be a big deal, but it was every place I went. This far away from any metropolis, food delivery services were non-existent and grocery delivery? Laughable. Yet, I needed these things and so I forced myself to go out. But my wall was cracking. I wasn't sure how much more I was going to be able to take.

And Beth wasn't helping the situation either. Our daily phone chats were more one-sided reasons for me to come home, and reminders how there was nothing for me in Cheshire Bay anymore. Put the house on the market, get a healthy return on it, and come back home having cleared my head and all that mumbo-jumbo she claimed was turning me into a weaker version of myself.

But I didn't feel weaker, on the contrary.

Yes, the murmurs were unnerving, but it didn't stop me from getting done what needed to be done. Yes, their words cut me like a knife, but none of them had been there that night. None of them understood how I harboured guilt for his death too. If I hadn't been popular, and I hadn't gotten it into my head how I was invincible, I wouldn't have climbed that cliff. I wouldn't have jumped, and Jordan would still be here. But on the whole, a strength inside was growing, and deep down, I knew I was capable of standing on my own without needing anybody.

Well, until today when the damn table wedged in the door.

Eric drank his coffee on the deck in an oddly comfortable peace, and although I wanted to inquire into his past, I let it be. Maybe he'd tell me. Besides, it wasn't like I was offering up tidbits. Parker's incessant rings still went unanswered, and I hadn't divulged anything more personal than him emptying his drawer. Aside from my mini rant on the second day, I'd stayed as tight lipped as Eric.

"Would you look at that?" He rose and stretched again, something on the horizon capturing his attention.

From my vantage point, however, I wasn't checking out the waves; I was admiring his rippled abs.

"I should get out there and tackle the waves. Would be an awful shame to pass them up. Sure you don't want to come out?"

I rubbed my belly. "Probably best that I don't."

With more grunting than was lady like, I pushed myself out of the seat. Guess Adirondack chairs were no longer suitable, as once I got in them, they were impossible to get out of, and I hadn't even grown to max size yet.

"If you change your mind, come hang out on the beach. It'll be good for you to relax a while."

Hmm. It was an intriguing idea. I hadn't actually done a lot of relaxing since I'd arrived. "Let me see what I can get done. I wouldn't mind getting my feet wet, but I still have a lot of work to do."

"I'd ask if you want help, but I think you'd refuse any and all offers of help." He winked.

"Yeah, well the table is no longer wedged, thanks to you. Sanding and painting is the easy part."

"Call me when it's ready to move back. I'll make that even easier."

I took the mug from him, and it clanged against mine when I looped them through my finger. "Have fun. Ride a big one for me."

I'd hoped the green-eyed monster threatening to control my voice faded.

The sanding was relatively easy, all things considered, and the first coat of paint went on well. But the crashing waves were distracting, and the hollers from the surfers on the sea scratched my soul. As the paint dried, I went up to my room and surveyed the ocean. The swells were gorgeous, and coloured dots of surfers rode the waves into shore. A deep longing in my soul beckoned me back to the sea. Back in the day, I'd been pretty decent and could hold my own on my board. Nothing flashy, of course, but enough that it was a healthy mix of adrenaline and relaxation.

From my vantage point, I studied my neighbour. Eric was a great surfer to watch. He had incredible strength as he paddled out to catch the big one, and a natural balance on the board as he became one with the current. He was mesmerizing and hot to watch. His wet suit hid nothing, and I allowed dirty thoughts to drift into places they had no right to visit.

However, sexy times were over. My expanding waistline was a major turnoff, and was an incredible form of birth control, especially since no one would touch me anyway. When the baby arrived, any lingering desires would be kiboshed. Completely. Yep, the moment Parker walked away, that was the end of my sex life.

Chapter Eight

For the next two weeks, I attacked my place with renewed energy. The cupboard doors came off and were given a light sanding and a paint job. As an interesting bonus, I'd found another inscription underneath a drawer. Dad sure loved leaving his mark on the place.

At first, on Beth's suggestions, I swore she'd made a mistake in her colour choices, but once I had the doors back in place, I had to admit, it gave a brand-new look and feel to the place. With the table back in place, the kitchen had a modern and bright appearance, while at the same time suited the environment.

If I went forward with my plans to rent it out in the fall, I was sure it wouldn't be long before I could find a suitable guest. If I went that way. I had the ad all drafted and ready, and selected the best site to host it on. However, the more time I spent fixing it up, the more I wanted to keep it all to myself, but on the flip side of that coin, I also knew I couldn't live here full time. Not with the baby. Cheshire Bay wasn't for raising families, just visiting with them.

Besides, while I was painting and sanding, menial work I originally despised, I found myself rather enjoying it. I was no interior decorator, and left those ideas to Beth, but I enjoyed running the little sander, and seeing the results from the effort I'd put into my work lit me up in a way I didn't expect. Such a change from sitting in an office all day, typing away.

While the days kept me busy, the nights were a little quieter. Every so often, I'd sit on the back porch with my sexy as hell neighbour. Eric had a beer and talked about some of his more interesting passengers, and the places he visited on the island. It was a friendly environment, a safe space. No one brought up my past and it actually wasn't given a whole lot of worry either. On the back deck, I was free to be me.

"Hey," Eric called over his deck, across the small strip of space between us and into my kitchen. "It's going to be a hot one, and I strongly suggest you keep cool today."

"You just can't wait to see me in a bikini, right?" Thank god it came out in a whisper. My hormones had no self-control.

"Why don't you come in the water today?"

Because I'm a whale? I gave my stretched-out skin a rub. I was thirty-three weeks pregnant, and my belly now sported its own zip code, even if the local family doctor assured me everything was okay. He wasn't as sweet and kind as my doctor back home was, but since it was just a quick checkup, it was tolerable. However, the heat was pressing on me and even just dipping my toes in the ocean would be a welcome reprieve from the heat.

"You know what, maybe I'll just get my feet wet."

The humidity was rising rapidly, and the marine forecast predicted a doozy of a storm. Probably why all the surfers were back in town and riding the waves down at long beach, where the waves would be bigger. On our edge of the coastline, the swells were pretty decent here and a novice boarder could still have a good time.

"You don't want to overheat, remember?" Eric had been a good friend to lean on when I overworked myself and gave the best back and shoulder massages.

"Fine." The cooling down would help me focus, as I needed to start coming up with a business plan. With no job and a baby on the way, the buyout wasn't going to last forever. As it was, I was still paying rent on an apartment I hadn't seen in over a month. "I'll be out there in a little bit."

Eric nodded and disappeared back into his house.

I was heading up to my room when my phone rang,

75

Beth's face showing on the display.

"Hey."

"Listen, I don't have much time to talk."

I rolled my eyes. Typical.

"I'm coming in for an overnight visit. Booked myself a little charter as the company's paying for it, since we can do a shoot for the local magazine on beach house renovations. Should be there on Saturday. Does that work for you?"

"Your room's been made up for some time just waiting for the perfect guest." I sighed and rummaged through my drawer, finding a bikini bottom. I lifted it up wondering if it would even cover my hips anymore.

"Fine. Did you get the pano?"

"Yesterday. I hung it up and you're right, it looks great."

It was a sunset view from the water looking in towards the shore, the windows reflecting the orange of the sun – the pop of colour Beth said I needed. I'm positive if I could zoom in on it, the houses dotting the water's edge were of my bay.

"Told you it would work." Her nails clicked against her keyboard. "I got to run, meeting with one of the Jonas' brothers at his rental in an hour. Saturday. Noon. Pick me up from the airport?"

"I'll be there."

"See you then." She hung up without another word.

I got longer goodbyes from the hardware people than I did my best friend. I brushed off feelings niggling at the back of my head. Beth was busy, the quintessential city girl always on the run. Had I changed that much over the month that her clipped tones were grating my nerves? Nah, it had to be pregnancy induced. According to the book, I was at that stage where I was quickly agitated.

And also easily turned on.

I stood naked in my bedroom, running my hands over my filled-out body. My boobs were bigger and had a bit of weight to them as I cupped them. Just holding them caused the nipples to harden and pop out. But the biggest surprise was how thinking about Eric caused my lower body to tingle and ache. There would be nothing between us, as I'd pushed away his advances, but that didn't stop the fantasy from playing out wildly in my head and ending with a little personal time.

There was something freeing about being naked, at least in the privacy of my own home. Eric was out on the water, so I was in no rush to get dressed and even walked out on to the newly finished floor on the balcony off my bedroom. The sun was nice, and the breeze cooled my body, but only on the surface. A mental image of my neighbour–topless–working on my cupboard doors floated through my mind and fired up the embers of desire. I needed to get into the water and cool down pronto.

I located a bikini top with enough coverage to not be considered slutty but with enough support that I didn't get uniboob, threw my hair in a top knot, grabbed a towel and made my way out to the beach. How crazy was it that I'd been here for a month already, and this would be my first dip in the water since my arrival? When I was a kid, it would've been fifteen minutes max before I was dripping wet.

I stretched out my towel and sat upon it, my hands supporting me as I leaned back soaking up the sunshine and watched the surfers from behind my oversized sunglasses while a deep ache still nestled between my legs. I should've taken care of business before coming down.

Eric lined up perfectly with me and rode the waves like he was an all-star surfing champ, and who knows, maybe he was. Since that first week, neither of us talked about the past, or the years in between my visits to the bay.

Board under his arm, he walked within a couple feet of my towel. Water ran in rivulets down his bright green wetsuit and made puddles as he stood along the edge of the wet sand.

"Hope you're wearing sunscreen?"

"Nah. I tan well. Haven't burnt yet." It was a genetic gift, and even though I was sporting more of a tank top tan than my teenage years of bikini straps would've liked, my skin was a decent bronzed colour. Aside from the sun-reflecting belly.

"You should regardless."

And you could run it all over me.

I tore my gaze away. What was wrong with me? Eric and I were friends. I was leaving in a month to go home. There simply couldn't be anything. He wasn't likely interested in screwing a pregnant chick; there was too much belly in the way. Besides that, he said last time he simply read too much into situations, so he wasn't interested, only reacting to the feelers I was putting out, which wasn't much if I controlled myself.

I breathed in a long breath of salty sea air and listened to the waves lap against the beach. "Tell you what, if I feel my skin warming up, I'll take a dip." But as I said it, I was feeling warm already.

Maybe it was the way Eric's eyes roamed across me, taking in my partially covered body. Maybe it was because the sky was cloudless and the sun beat its energy, having no mercy. Whatever it was, my body was heating up, the ache between my legs intensified into a low throb, and the flicker of desire in Eric's dark eyes didn't help.

"You know what, maybe I will go for a swim now." I rolled myself to a stand, and before I got on my feet, Eric extended his hand, which I gratefully took. "Can't wait to see how much of a whale I'll be when I'm due."

"I'm sure you'll still be beautiful." He turned his head away quickly.

My heart thrummed in my chest, but I didn't know how to respond to his statement. Instead, he let go of my hand and allowed me to lead the way into the water. The ocean was cool and sent an intense shiver of goosebumps over my body, but even though it was only my feet fully immersed, my body started to cool down. Thank goodness, now if it only worked to dull the ache. Slowly, I inched my way in, bending over and splashing the sea up my legs.

"Not too far." A warning clicked on the edge of Eric's tongue. "The undertow is quite strong this year."

"Then I'll sit here." Gasping breathlessly as my fire-hot centre splashed into the cool water, I shuddered a breath. The push and pull of the tide was mesmerizing, and I found myself leaning back further on my arms, as they were slowly enveloped into the wet sand. Eventually, I was far enough back my head was floating. I smiled at Eric as he looked down on me. It was soul lifting to be back in the water.

As I lay there floating, I gauged the changing expression on his face. His eyes sailed over my body again but settled on the bald island poking above the water, just as my little one sent out a noticeable kick. His eyes grew large.

"Want to feel?" I sat up, watching as the belly

island sunk back into the ocean.

"I... I..." He searched my face and I reached for his hand, hovering it above the last movement. "Ya, sure." With that, I pressed his hand against the side of my belly and the little one responded with a karate chop. "Wow, that's really cool."

I cherished watching his expression. For weeks now, I'd been feeling movement, and it made me happy to see someone other than me get a kick out of it. But it had been a bad idea. Just having his hand on me fired up the dormant butterflies, and the pounding of my heart had to have given a jolt of energy to the baby as it started step-dancing over my bladder.

"Does it do that all the time?" His eyes remained large and focused.

"Mostly at night. During the day, he's pretty silent."

"He?"

"It's just what I call it. Seems wrong to me to address it as an it. Some days it's she, today it's he."

"You have no idea?"

I shrugged. "None. And none of those dreams either. Some women get a strong idea about what they're having, I haven't had any thoughts one way or another."

He left his hand on my belly, inching it a little to the left or right, presumable to chase down the movements, and I doubted I would've complained had he moved further south. "That's really nifty." He winked as he said the last word. "Thanks for sharing."

I gazed into his eyes, noting for the first time how deep they were, the colour of wet sand under the moonlight, and try as I may, I couldn't tear myself away. My gaze searched out the laugh lines on his face, and I lowered my gaze to study his full lips.

It had to be hormones, pure and simple. There was no other acceptable reason. The hormones made me horny, desperately horny, and Eric being the sweet, sexy guy he was had become my body's focus. The truth was I was on my own for the pregnancy and the rest of my life, and I was prepared to fully take it on. I knew I could manage. But seeing Eric stare into my eyes, it had me wanting to rip his wetsuit off his body and take him right there on the beach.

Instead, I moved my lips closer to his while he slowly lowered his head.

In a heartbeat, our lips crashed together, at first, teasing the other out as if asking for permission, and then diving in fully, tongues intertwined as we locked our lips together.

It was a good thing I was in the water as his kiss was so powerful, it heated me to a level I never knew existed, and had I been standing it had the intensity to weaken my knees. Just before I was out of air, he pulled away, a heat and hunger yearning in his eyes I'd wanted to see for the rest of my life. He stared into my soul like no one had before. I'd just shared a deeper intimacy with him as he touched my belly and kissed the life out of my lips than I had with Parker. How did that even happen? How was that even possible?

I splashed some water over my chest and arms, unable to speak or utter a sound, but I couldn't stop looking at him. And the smile on his face never faded. My heart skipped a beat as my brain sounded an alarm, warning me I was leaving in four weeks.

Chapter Nine

"Do you feel up to surfing?" Eric stood impossibly close, as he held his surfboard in front of him.

We stood at the edge of the water, shoulder to shoulder, waves slapping against my thighs. "I want to, but I don't think I could paddle out since I can't lay on my stomach." My hands ran around the swell of my belly.

"You could frog lay. Would that help?" He passed me his board.

"I don't think so."

I hadn't accepted the board fully, yet. I really wanted to try, but I was sure I'd be unable to get out far enough to enjoy the ride in. And popping up? That could be an issue since I hadn't in years and my balance wasn't what it used to be, thanks to the baby throwing off my centre of gravity.

"I'll swim out beside you. You don't have to go out far. I can see the desire in your eyes to at least give it a shot."

The desire was more than just for the possibility of surfing, it was for the handsome guy offering me the opportunity. This time, I jumped at the chance. It had to be like riding a bike, right? I balanced on the board, trying to find a position to lay in that allowed me to paddle. The frog pose was the most awkward, with my boobs flattened against the board and my rear end up in the air, giving an undignified view to Eric who swam behind me. I didn't get very far out before I called it quits, fighting to catch my breath. "I give up." Maybe if I'd been doing it my whole pregnancy, it would be natural, but this was beyond odd.

"Aw, too bad, I enjoyed the perspective." He swam to the front of the board and put his arms on, resting his chin on top.

Breathlessly, I rolled up and straddled the board, my legs dangling in the water and checked out how far I'd managed to go out. Our houses dotted the landscape, and I could still see the towel I'd hung on the upstairs banister. "Come up, sit with me. Rest."

Eric managed to hop on the head of the board without tipping us into the water and slid his way closer while we floated and breathed and basked in the sun.

Together we bobbed with the motion of the ocean,

slowly drifting towards land. The sun heated my chest and warmed my skin as I held the foot of the board behind my back.

"God, you're gorgeous."

I tipped my head up to look him straight in the eyes. "You're pretty damn handsome yourself."

His voice lowered to a deep and sexy level. "I'd love to take you right here on my board." The sexy way he was devouring my body turned me on, again.

"What?" My voice cracked. No way that could happen. I've done many things on a surfboard, but never that. As turned on as I was by the prospect...

"Interested?"

Yes, but no way. I shook my head but slowly inched my body closer, curious how this would work. He was in a wetsuit for crying out loud.

Eric wrapped his hand around my head and brought me in for a kiss, igniting the lingering embers into a full-on fire. "Lean back again, the way you were at first, and tip your head back."

I gripped the board with both hands and glanced around. We were pretty much on our own out here.

"Don't move or you'll tip us."

My curiosity was piqued, and my core was smoldering with deep tingles and desires. The carnal ache had only grown stronger. He hadn't yet touched me, and I was ready to come apart.

He trailed a finger over my collarbone and dipped into the space between my heaving boobs. My breath hitched, and I stared him deep in the eyes. One at a time, he cupped them, maintaining perfect balance.

"Oh god." I moaned, proving it had been a while since I'd been touched by a man.

"I haven't even begun."

A charming smile spread across his face as a cool finger trickled down over my heated bump, circling around it and teasing its way lower. Both of his hands braced against my hips, and slowly, tenderly, he caressed my thighs, moving in deeper with each pass. Instinctively, I opened for him, giving him access to what desperately needed attention.

"Lean back further." His voice was hoarse with desire.

Oh Lord, I threatened to rip apart as he slipped a finger under my bottoms, pushing the material off to the side, and dipping right into the heated heart of me. I closed my eyes and allowed the soaring sensations to control my body as he slowly touched and tenderly caressed and expertly moved his fingers, creating breathless gasps of air and involuntary shudders. My fingers dug into the edges of the board as my body surrendered to Eric, and one wave of ecstasy after another crashed over me. My body twitched and threatened to flip us both. However, the moment passed, and he retracted his hand, while I pushed up and wrapped my arms around him. Beneath his wetsuit, the hardest part of him pressed into my belly and a need to ride him like a surfboard overtook me.

"How fast can we get back to shore?" I begged, my voice raw and carnal.

To hell with waiting. If I was going to be here for only a few weeks more, I may as well enjoy myself.

After a rousing afternoon, I pushed my hair off my face as I opened my eyes and took in the surroundings of Eric's bedroom. There was a little pop-up table beside me with a bottle of water and a note tucked under it.

Drink this, you need rehydration. I'm downstairs on the patio.

I collected my two bikini pieces and got dressed, heading downstairs. My itch had been scratched, and I was feeling less randy than before. Better than that thought, was a feeling of being on top of the world and utterly relaxed.

"How long was I asleep?" I twisted the cap off and took a long sip, relishing the cool water sliding down my throat.

"A couple of hours." His focus was on the sea.

"Oh, wow. I'm sorry."

I hadn't meant to fall asleep at all, but I guess I was so played out it just happened. I grabbed my towel hanging on the edge of the deck and wrapped it around since Eric was no longer in his wetsuit or buck naked in all his incredible glory and was instead dressed in shorts and a tee.

He set down a plate filled with grape stems and made to get up. "You hungry?"

"Famished." A buffet would not be out of place, and although people would likely stare at me, I could blame the growing baby.

"Care to go out and have a bite to eat? You haven't been to Birch Bay Burgers, have you?"

I shook my head as he rose, lightly patting his shoulder. "No."

He twisted away from my touch and focused his attention on his wet suit hanging on the hook and flipped it around, preoccupied it seemed with anything but me. "That settles it. Can you be ready in an hour?"

"Sure." Should I give him a playful little kiss or not? His attitude was so different from our afternoon together. "Thanks for the water." I stepped onto the first stair and stared at him as if by standing there half-dressed he'd come to his senses and at least throw me a smile or something.

I stood there, tightening the grip on my towel wondering what had changed between us while I'd slept.

Before I'd closed my eyes, everything was euphoric, and our orgasms were out of this world, at least mine were. It had been the best afternoon I'd had since coming back to Cheshire Bay.

"See you in a bit." An unsettled wave of despair in my soul roared to life with his quick dismissal.

Just before my ex walked out on me and the baby, he'd given me the cold shoulder too. Said he needed time to think about how his future was going to change abruptly, as he was way too young to be a father and at his age, he should be hanging out with his buddies, not changing diapers.

The way Eric kept his distance brought up that same current of trepidation.

Chapter Ten

*A*n hour later, smelling less like sex and ocean and sadness, and more like lilacs blooming on a spring day, I knocked on Eric's door. Gone was the darkness, his eyes twinkled at the sight of me decked out in a maxi dress, and I was grateful for the emerging smile and the way he bent down and lifted my hand, delicately kissing my knuckles.

He helped me into his car, and we drove off, taking the winding road south to another bay. I kept my window rolled down and let the fresh air smack me in the face since the switchbacks he drove at a high speed made me nauseous.

Birch Bay Burgers was perched on a rocky outcropping complete with a 300-degree view of the Pacific. It was on the fancier end of places to eat, given its isolated location, but in the grand scheme of things, it was still a burger joint.

Our server sat us beside a railing, where along with the amazing panoramic view, we also had a symphony of waves crashing against the rocks beneath us. In the far southernly distance, a storm battled as flickers of light danced along the horizon. The air was also a little chillier, so I was grateful I'd brought a sweater and I pulled it tighter around my shoulders.

"Thank you for this afternoon. I couldn't have had a better day," I started out saying, after taking a sip of water. Aside from cheap small talk and one-word answers to my questions, there hadn't been much conversation on the way here.

"Yeah, the waves were perfect."

A low rumble of thunder sounded in the distance.

I swallowed down the bitter taste of bile rapidly forming in the back of my throat. "Eric, have I done something wrong?"

Finally, he focused on me. "No. Why do you ask?"

"I don't know, you just seem... Distant." Like you got what you needed from me and you're ready to toss me in the garbage.

He puffed out his chest but turned to view the surf smacking the rocks. "Can I be honest with you?"

Rising bitterness bubbled in my gut. "I hope you will be. I need that." Oh, how I needed people to be honest with me, rather than whisper behind my back.

"I'm very confused."

I wrung my hands together on my lap. "About?" A part of me was confused as well since I couldn't pin down Eric and his flipping emotions.

"About you and about me." The breeze floated by and rippled the collar of his unbuttoned shirt as he lowered his chin.

A gust of air sailed out of me. "I'm not sure I follow."

"You said you didn't want anything from me, and you pushed back against my advances, and yet today, you kissed me, and we had the best sex ever multiple times."

Although he kept his voice low enough for only me to hear, I still couldn't help myself and I searched out the nearby patrons to see if anyone overheard. If they did, they didn't act like it. "What's happening between us… it's complicated."

"I can uncomplicate it. Real quick."

The finality in his tone worried me and raised alarms that I had been right in my quick assumption. Eric knew I was an easy score back in the day, and now that he got it, he was through with me. He'd taken some time to do it, but he'd cracked my defenses and entered my heart. And now, he was confused? What was there to be confused about?

I tipped my head and pressed into the back of my chair, unsure of which direction was the best one to take. "I like you; I really do. I think you're a very sweet guy."

And it was more than that, but I wasn't ready to completely voice anything more. An overwhelming feeling of being dumped by a guy I wasn't even going out with threatened to undo the last vestiges of my strength.

"And here comes the giant but."

"Not at all." My foot nervously tapped against the table pedestal. "The thing is…" No matter how I wanted to continue the sentence, there was going to be a *but* or a *however*. Damn, I hated when a guy was right. "The thing is…" I sighed again because it hit me, like a bolt of lightning.

Eric hadn't used me - I'd been the one doing the using. He satisfied my itch, just like the others had done when I was fifteen. Only this time, instead of being only momentarily hurt by their rejection, I was feeling it on a whole other level because… I inhaled sharply. Somewhere along the lines, I'd developed feelings for Eric, which wasn't at all fair to him. I was a package deal, baby, and all, and he didn't need that.

"I'm only here for the summer, and I'm not even sure if I'm going to be here that long. Coming back to Cheshire Bay was to clear my system and redo the old beach house. Make it ready to rent out to someone else. I knew when I arrived, my being here wasn't a permanent thing." There I said it. "Besides, everywhere I go, people still talk."

Yes, there had been a momentary reprieve when a celebrity appeared in town, but after that, the gossip was still there. The dirty looks, the whispers. It was getting old.

"It's a small town."

"With small town mentality. They'll never forgive me, and they definitely will never forget."

"Lily, you painted over the town's name and made a fool out of yourself."

Not one of my finest moments, but in the end, I owned up to it and spent the next two days scrubbing the paint off.

"Most kids go through a rebellion of sorts, but you, it was like you were out for blood. You were…" He paused and leaned in closer. "An absolute lunatic. And no one can forget that."

I hung my head as the town proved just how much they hadn't forgotten over the past few weeks.

Eric kept going. "At the height of your past, there was Jordan. One of us. Who died?" He didn't need to follow it up with *because of you.*

A knife to my heart, it twisted and carved, breaking me in a way I'd never dealt with. Just thinking about that incident soured my stomach. "I'm very much aware, but I didn't kill him."

Wicka was a small island in the northern bay. You needed a boat to drive to the far side, and I had managed to find a group of guys willing to take me. After a few drinks, and a couple of doobies, I accepted a dare, and then a double dare from the guy I'd just screwed. Without hesitation, I climbed up to the top of a cliff, with Jordan licking my heels. We both stood at the top breathless, staring down at the dark water while the seven friends chanted below. Then we jumped.

I was fearless back then, and completely foolish and naïve. And also lucky. Damn lucky. I survived the jump, having not checked for any jagged ridges of rocks hidden deep under the water.

Unfortunately for Jordan, who was easily double my weight, lady luck was not with him. He died instantly when he cracked into the rocks, a rock slicing him open from pelvis to chest. He bled out before we found him.

Rumours circulated that it was my fault, and had I not jumped in the first place, the kid wouldn't have jumped either. After that, at least until I stopped coming around, the area was put under patrol. There wasn't much danger in anyone going back anyway. No one wanted to be around Jordan's ghost.

Understandably, it put a total damper on the end of summer festivities and parents were strongly encouraged to keep a better eye on their kids, which meant I wasn't allowed out of eyesight. Until those eyes couldn't stay awake anymore, then I was a free bird. Looking back on my time, I wasn't a great person.

It hurt that Eric brought it up, how he sat there immune to the turmoil raging inside of me.

My voice cracked, and I pleaded with all I had in me. "I didn't force Jordan to jump. For crying out loud, it was a dare. He didn't have to take it." A fresh set of tears blurred my vision. "But you know what, I've paid for that mistake over and over again, even though I had nothing to do with it." A tampered down rage was building inside of me. "My dad was forced out of town, maybe not in a physical sense, but in a mental one. No one wanted to help him with any projects, his business here derailed, and he had to deal with a rebellious teenager who wanted nothing more than to be loved, and who hunted for alternate ways of getting that need met."

I'd found a way to get it too. It was always with the guy who showed me the most affection, and after we'd had a quick fix, we'd share a doobie around a campfire, and he'd ignore me having gotten what he needed. You think I would've learned. But no. It went on that whole summer, until Jordan jumped. Then I had no one.

I stared across the small table at the man before me. Even twelve years later, what happened? I had sex with the guy who lavished his attention on me, and same thing happened. He was pushing me away now that he'd had his fix and reminding me of everything I did wrong. All this time, I'd thought Eric was different.

Instead of saying anything, he leaned back in his chair and surveyed the change in the atmosphere. The air was getting thick with humidity from the approaching storm, and there was a chill breezing over my way.

I leaned back and crossed my legs, keeping my back to the others in the restaurant, debating if I should stay or leave. Leaving was the easy way out but staying with someone who believed the worst about me wasn't really a better option, especially when I played right into his goal.

Lure her in with sweetness, have some mind-blowing sex, and ditch the bitch.

For a while, I believed I was special, and for a time, I'd considered staying in Cheshire Bay and seeing what could become of us.

How stupid and foolish I had been to hope there would ever be anything more, even if deep down it was all a pipe dream.

"Listen." I inhaled and crossed my arms over my chest. Everything inside was hurting, and my heart was breaking in pieces. "That summer was the worst one of my life, and if I could change it, I would in a heartbeat. I did a lot of dreadful things, and I wasn't a great friend. I wasn't even a good person." I searched his eyes which were locked on me. At least he was listening.

"But I'm not that same person. Not completely. I still want the same things – to be loved and to be accepted, and I'm definitely not going to ever find that here." My best bet was to sell the house, and like Beth said, tuck my tail between my legs and come home. Oh, how right she'd been. It had been a giant mistake coming back. "I'm sorry, Eric. I'm sorry you knew me back then, and I'm sorry you can't see that I've changed." I rummaged through my purse and pulled out some cash, dropping it on the table as I rose.

"Lily, wait…"

Tears fell down my face. "I'm sorry."

He turned his head away.

I hailed an uber, and on the way back to my place and texted Beth. "It's on."

Chapter Eleven

I was in a mood to fight.

The ride home did nothing to settle me down. I didn't want to cry anymore, I wanted to punch something, or better yet, yell and scream until I had no energy remaining and felt all my anguish was gone. My key nearly bent from being stabbed into the lock repeatedly. After twisting it open, I stepped inside and slammed the door shut.

The loud staccato beats of the *Imperial March* sounded.

Duh duh duh, DUN DA DUN, DUN DA DUN

For once, Parker's timing didn't stink. Gloves on and blood already boiled, I was ready.

"What do you want?" I barked into the speaker as I stormed up the stairs to the master bedroom.

"Finally, you answered." There was a time when hearing his voice once soothed me, but now the very sound of his Newfie-ish accent grated my last remaining nerves.

"What do you want?"

"I want to see you again. Where are you? You haven't been home in a month."

My heart stopped beating despite the quick cardio workout. "What do you mean? I had the locks changed." Two days before I left for Cheshire Bay, three weeks after he walked away from us.

"Yeah, and thanks for the heads up on that. I had to ask the super."

I braced myself against the wall and inhaled sharply. "And he gave you a set?" I'd been pretty clear when I had the locks changed the reasoning behind that. It seemed my next call to make was to the superintendent of my building to give him a solid piece of my mind.

"Of course. Johnny and I go way back."

Fantastic. They were likely comic book buddies or something. The blood in my veins chilled faster than the air around me as I entered my master suite. I'd left all the windows open, and in desperation to feel warm and secure, I slammed them shut and quickly raced to the unlocked patio door.

"So where are you, Babe?"

"Not with you."

"Right? Our bed is so cold without you."

Ew. He's still sleeping in my bed, in my apartment,

even though I wasn't there. The ethics and violations being smashed left and right were upping the anxiety levels in me. Dizziness was settling in, and I needed to sit down. The first available space was the deck chair on the balcony.

"I went to your office."

My mouth dried in an instant and even a quick swallowing did nothing. My legs weakened. I wanted to throw up.

"Why didn't you tell me you got fired?"

I was given a buyout, not fired. Although it didn't really matter. No doubt my perfume was still lingering in the air when they removed my name from the door. I grasped the arm rest of the chair and slid into it.

The karate kid was waking up and stretched, pushing against my dress with a noticeable bump. I rubbed it until it smoothed out, trying to calm myself down. But it wasn't working. The longer the air cackled between Parker and I, the harder my heart pounded.

Parker was in my apartment. He'd been to my work. What else was he capable of?

"You know, since you haven't been home or to work, I've been trying to figure out where you are."

A cold sweat built across the back of my neck.

"And that's when I had a moment of brilliance."

The audacity of Parker having any smarts was laughable. What had I ever seen in the guy? He was gorgeous and amazing in bed, but other than that? He had an entry level position with a marketing company and zero desire to move up. He spent his free time–

"So, I contacted Beth."

I laughed. "As if she'd tell you anything."

"You're right, she refused all my calls." His breathing was heavy, calculating, and it caused the hairs to stand upright on the back of my sweaty neck. "Turns out she's away this weekend. Catching a flight to the island?"

A weight of a thousand nightmares sat on my chest, rendering me speechless. I gazed across to Eric's house, as one by one the lights flickered to life. Thank god he was home. Knowing that meant the world to me.

"So, I did some more digging."

A bolt of lightning flashed across the sky, the static echoing over the phone before a clap of thunder nearly rendered me deaf. Long gone was the fight instinct, instead it had been replaced by the flight portion. I pushed the end button and stormed back into my house, securing the patio door.

I checked the guest suite and bathroom, ensuring all windows were closed and locked tight with the lights all on, before heading downstairs and repeating my security check there. After a long while of pacing, which did nothing to calm my racing heart, I finally gave up and sat on the couch.

Maybe Parker had been baiting me, hoping to find out where I was? Beth sure as hell wouldn't tell him, and it was unlikely her admin would've said anything.

It should've put me at ease, but it didn't. It only made things worse.

A deep vibration rumbled under my cheek, and I blinked myself awake. My phone buzzed again, and I pulled away my hand, the phone still tightly gripped in my hand. It wasn't the *Imperial March*, so I hit the answer button.

"Where are you?"

I shot up and rubbed my crusty eyes to read the name on the display. "Beth?" My throat was raw, as if I'd swallowed razor blades.

"I'm about to board the plane to you. You still going to pick me up?"

I coughed to clear away the frog. "That was today?"

"Yes."

The note of distain in her voice was a little too much for me, especially since I'd yet to have a coffee and had managed a few shitty hours of sleep, if I were being generous.

"When do you land?"

"Forty-five minutes?"

"I'll be there. Don't you worry." She hung up

before I had the chance to say goodbye. It wasn't much time to get ready, but it would be enough.

I gave a quick glance to Eric's house, wondering what kind of night he'd had. His lights shut off before midnight, and a couple of times he made it out onto the deck but retreated after a few breaths. I managed to sneak out onto my own back porch for a moment, hiding in the shadows as he glanced over to my place. Sadness settled over his features, but I wasn't too upset by that. He deserved it for bringing up my past and throwing it in my face.

Was he going to be Beth's pilot? It was a good thing they didn't know who the other was, Beth would make his flight unbearable. Normally, that would've made me smile, but now, it caused untold worry.

Eric wasn't a bad guy, the opposite in fact. He'd been the first one to welcome me back, and to make Cheshire Bay a home. He was a reason for me to stay and enjoy my time here. Without asking, he'd helped me settle in and offered his hand, and his heart, more than once. But like everyone else, he couldn't let my past go.

Why did things need to be so complicated?

I pulled up outside the green building, only slightly bigger than three of the beach houses combined; hardly airport sized. Pacing outside and fanning myself as the humidity levels were reaching the unbearable stage, I headed into the air-conditioned building for reprieve.

I wasn't three steps in, when a voice called out.

"Welcome to Pacific... Hey, Lily."

Eric's friend from the bonfires strutted by. "Hi, Cedar."

She hopped out from around her little desk and gave me a big hug. "How's it going? Look at you, so full of life." Her hands hovered over my belly and the scarf she wore, loosened as she bent over. "How's the baby?"

"Good. Do you want to feel? He's not moving much right now."

Her eyes grew as large as saucers as she placed her hands on either side of the bump. "Are you here to see Eric? He's on final approach."

"No, not Eric." I avoided her eye contact. "However, he is bringing a friend of mine over."

"Oh, okay." A door behind us opened. "Mitchy," she yelled, and I pulled my head back from the volume. "Guess who's here?"

Mitch emerged from the door, dressed in coveralls. His hands were black with engine dirt and grease. "Hey, if it isn't Miss Lily." He walked over and carefully, without touching me, air-kissed each cheek. "Are you here for–"

"Nah," Cedar jumped in, saving me from any explanation. "Her friend's on the 145."

"Bonfire tonight?" he asked, flipping a hopeful

gaze from Cedar to me.

I shook my head and glanced around. "I'll politely decline since I have company."

Mitch waved his hand in the air. "Whatever. Bring them along. No one's going to mind, and you know there's always enough food."

I nodded at the truth. "I make no promises."

"Fair enough." He looked over my shoulder, and I turned just in time. Eric set the plane down perfectly on the runway. "145. Touchdown."

"It's okay." Cedar pointed to the wall of windows. "Once the plane stops, you can go out there. Just tell them you're with Eric and no one will give you any hassle."

With Eric. My heart constricted. *Don't I wish?*

After Cedar's prodding, I inched my way to the door, and simply watched. At the end of the runway, the plane turned, and taxied its way toward the building. The plane was much bigger than I thought, like something out of a movie, and it was cool watching it drive right up and stop about fifty feet from the door. No way that was ever happening in any major city.

The stairs unfolded and a couple of minutes later, Beth stood at the top of the steps shaking her perfectly styled bob. The epitome of business, she was dressed as though she'd just left the office after meeting another high-profile client - pencil skirt, blazer, and high heels. She stuck out like a sore thumb as she made her way onto the tarmac and over to the belly of the place where the luggage doors were opening.

Two more passengers ventured off the plane after her, but they didn't capture my attention like the last man did.

Eric stood at the top, wearing aviators and a captain's hat, dressed nicely in a crisp blue shirt and khakis. He had more of a professional but laid-back style than my friend who was currently barking orders at a young baggage handler.

"Damn." I stepped outside and kept my head down but stayed within touching distance of the building. The overpowering scent of jet-fuel turned my stomach.

Mitch walked by me. "You can come out further."

"I'm good here. I'll wait for her to get her belongings." I expected Beth would have an overnight bag. I did not expect a small crate plus two giant suitcases. She was only staying the one night.

She wheeled her luggage over to me and dropped the handles to give me a solid once over. "Look at you." She touched my belly before I had the chance to offer. "You're so huge."

"Thanks."

She ran a perfectly manicured finger down my cheek. "I thought pregnant women slept lots. You look like you haven't slept since you got here. I bet it's because you missed me, and your old life."

"Rough night, and yes I do miss you. Listen, I need to talk…" My voice faded away as she continued to speak over me.

"Gawd, Lil. You should've told me you needed some clothes. I would've grabbed some from that boutique you like. I'm sure they must have maternity clothes, or at least something in a bigger size."

She eyed me up and down.

"This is new."

It was a beautiful maxi dress in a nice linen material. It was airy and light and had lots of room for expansion. I'd bought it from one of the shops on the main drag where, for the first time since getting here, they treated me like a customer and not a disease.

Her hand waved through the air. "When you come home, we'll go shopping at one of those upscale places, Boudoir et More, or whatever it's called." She passed me one of the luggage handles. "Here. Someone's going to bring over the crate, so we'll need to get to your vehicle."

"What's in the big box?"

I glanced over her shoulder where Eric stood at the base of the stairs, staring in my direction. The urge to walk over and say hi was strong, but after last night… It was best I let him go. Between Parker and things back in Vancouver, it was the better idea.

Beth carried on. "I brought a few things for the photo shoot. Nothing much since you've done really well with my suggestions and the beach home looks great. Your bag has all the camera equipment so be easy with it and don't let it drop."

One more time, I looked in Eric's direction.

"C'mon, Lily," Beth called out. "We've got work to do."

Head tipped down, I followed my friend back into the building. Work to do. Yes, that was the best phrase. And nothing like a ticking clock in which to put some urgency on it.

Chapter Twelve

I opened the door back into the airport's building and allowed Beth to go in first, following quickly behind her fast pace.

"See you tonight?" Cedar asked as I approached the front door, tugging a heavy suitcase.

"Maybe."

Beth screwed up her face when she turned and focused on me. "What's going on tonight?"

"There's a bonfire on the beach." I put a touch of energy into the sentence, even if it was pointless. I wasn't going to go, and Beth most certainly was not going to go. That involved sand and hotdogs, two things on her hate list.

"Fun times." Beth rolled her eyes.

I waved hopelessly at Cedar and chased after Beth, who was already pushing her way outside.

She stood beside my Jeep as I unlocked it, set her

suitcase on the floor in the backseat, and grabbed the one I rolled out, setting it on the other side. "Can you believe I'm actually here?"

I shook my head, and really took in my friend. "No, not really, but I'm glad you came."

"I talked with Archie late last night, and he thinks he may already have a buyer for your place, but he wants it a week from Monday. Would that work?"

"What?" When I told Beth last night I was seriously thinking about selling, I wasn't ready to pack up and leave in a few days. "Tell him no."

She dismissed my comment with a shrug. "With the improvements you've made, you're right. We can hold out and still get top dollar in the fall, but this whole thing could be behind you in a week if you play your cards right." She turned at the sound of a vehicle coming over. "Finally. Can you put the backseat down, Lil? We'll need room for the crate."

Surprised and flabbergasted by Beth's attitude, but in too much shock to do much about it, I did as she asked. Had Beth always been so bossy? Or was I just sensitive to it because I wasn't seeing her every day? Whatever it was, it put a new light on my friend, one I wasn't sure I liked.

Mitch drove and parked behind my jeep. "Special delivery." He laughed, but from the corner of my eye Beth shook her head.

I walked over to help him and stared at the massive crate, not 100% sure it would fit in my vehicle.

"What are you doing?" Mitch asked as I wrapped my hand around one of the handles. "You're not carrying this."

"Mitch, I can do it."

"Your friend can help."

"Yeah? Good luck with that," I whispered. Beth hadn't moved. "I'll need to do it when I get this home anyways." Besides, it wasn't as heavy as a sheet of plywood, and I'd managed that all on my own.

"Yeah, right. Just a sec." Mitch hopped into the building, and a minute later, he came out with Eric.

My mouth went as dry as cotton, and the air pressure pushed down a little harder as he sauntered over with Mitch, all the while taking me in.

"What's up?" Eric asked Mitch after making quick eye contact with me.

Damn, the hot sun released his spicy cologne into the air, wrapping around me like a hug. It was intoxicating.

"Help me load this into her vehicle please."

With ease, the two of them got it loaded, on its side after Beth gave the okay, tearing her eyes away from her phone for a couple of seconds to approve the move.

"Are you finished?" Mitch asked Eric, dusting off his hands.

"I have another late flight in an hour, grabbing passengers from YVR. Why?" A curious expression crossed his face and slowly his gaze flittered back in my direction.

A sudden panic rocked my core – was Parker on that flight?

"She's going to unload this at her place, alone." Mitch glared at Beth who was now talking on the phone. "And I don't think she should."

"Yeah." Eric faced me but kept his distance, hands twitching at his sides. "I'd love to assist."

"Thanks, man." Mitch gave a solid shoulder pat to his buddy and leaned closer to me, air-kissing my cheeks again. "See you tonight."

A low throaty noise rolled out of Eric, and he covered his mouth briefly. Ensuring Beth was still on the phone as Mitch drove away, he whispered, "Listen, about last night."

I didn't want to go there. Not here, not when my friend was a few feet away. "I can't. Sorry. I'm just here for my best friend."

"That's *your* friend?" Eric thumbed to Beth, who paced in front of the building, giving orders to two of her minions. "Doesn't seem your type."

Based on her behaviour, it was hard to admit as much, but I did. "She's been my best friend for years."

Beth strutted over and a huge smile popped up on her face. "Why, hello. I'm Beth Jeffries." She extended her hand. "We never got a chance to be properly introduced on the plane."

"Eric Morris." He shook her hand but kept his focus on me. "So, I'm to follow you home?"

"Oh, that's wonderful. Got to love these small towns, right, Lily? Everyone always so eager to help."

I half expected her to clap her hands in enthusiasm, but thankfully she didn't. "Well, shall we get going? Archie's expecting pictures by dinner and it'll take some time to set up the shoot, especially since I'm doing this single-handedly as you don't know the first thing about staging."

"I can learn if you teach me."

She cocked an eyebrow. "Darling, I'm here for less than twenty-four hours. I hardly have time. Let's go. This guy is waiting for us."

I tipped my head down and got into my vehicle.

Eric set the crate inside the living room and tipped his cap in my direction. "Anything else I can do for you?" There was sarcasm in his speech directed at Beth, but she was too busy opening the lid to have paid it any attention.

"No, no, thank you." She pulled out a huge painting

and admired it for a few heartbeats. "Are you flying me home tomorrow?"

"Yes, ma'am."

Her shoulders relaxed and a broad smile pushed up the apples of her cheeks. "Would you mind helping me put this crate back into her vehicle again in the morning? That would be so nice." Setting down the painting, she reached into her purse and pulled out some cash, sticking it into Eric's shirt pocket with a sly smile on her face.

It's one thing to tip a guy, it's entirely different to stick it in his shirt pocket like a stripper.

Eric retrieved the money and set it on the counter without even looking at the amount, a disgusted expression shadowed his face. "It's not a problem, Ms. Jeffries."

"And it won't be necessary." My eyes narrowed into slits when I turned to my friend. "Beth, you and I can easily load it up. It's not that heavy."

Honest to God, what was wrong with my friend? Had she always been like that and I was only noticing it now having been distanced from her, or was it because I was stressed out and overly anxious from a lack of sleep?

"He asked if there was anything else he could do." She shrugged. "Thank you again, and we'll see you in the morning." As if he were one of her staff, she dismissed him with a wave. "Now, Lil, as we're unpacking this, tell me more about this guy who's breaking your heart."

Eric's gaze snapped back to me and heat flooded my cheeks. "Let me see Eric to the door."

He stood there, his jaw slack. "About last night. We need to talk. I heard your phone call."

Eyes wide I shook my head and pushed him down the hall.

His dress shoes clacked against the tiles as he made his way back to the entrance, and a smidgen of sympathy filled his face. "Is there anything I should know or prepare for?" Sympathy – was that it? – filled his face.

There was so much I needed to explain about Parker, but my lips stayed firmly pressed together.

"I'll be home all evening. If you need anything, flash your lights."

My gaze stayed locked onto his. Did he already know the truth?

In a louder voice, after clearing his throat, he announces, "I'll come by before I go in, and I'll load that crate, don't you worry."

"It'll already be done." I gave him a soft smile. "Don't worry about it." Pushing my weight onto my left leg, I hung on the opened door.

"Lily?" A sing-songy tone mixed with attitude flitted down the short hall. "Are you coming? I need your help."

"Sorry, I need to go."

117

"Bonfire? We need to talk."

"Maybe."

"Lily?" Her voice suddenly grated on my nerves.

"Coming."

Eric walked back to his vehicle, but he turned back twice to see if I was still there. Had I read too much into our conversation last night at the restaurant? Had I overreacted?

Beth called out, again, and I sauntered back into my living room.

"Which do you like best?" She had three prints sitting around the living room.

None of them, but because they were all the same. Ocean themed. All one had to do was turn around and see the real ocean, so why should there be prints of it hanging in the living room?

I scrunched up my face. "Well…"

"It's just for the photo." She lifted each one and admired it. "Let's do a photo with each since I can't decide. Once I'm back in the office, I'll be able to see which suits the mood."

"You're the boss."

I sat on a bar stool, watching helplessly as my best friend picked up her phone and called a colleague. Together they discussed my living room and kitchen before she walked outside to stare at the back of the house and complain about the sand. Her remarks about the house being in great shape and the spectacular view warmed my heart. Once Archie's name rolled off her tongue, I knew she was chatting with a real estate guy, so I made us a late lunch.

Beth stormed up the stairs. "Where's the camera suitcase?" Her voice was low.

I pointed beside the couch, and with another quick bounce, she was back outside tugging the luggage behind her. Lunch was a yummy chicken Caesar salad, but I picked at it as Beth snapped photos of the living room, varying the pictures and placement of the minor decorations I'd kept around.

"Aren't you going to eat?" Her plate remained untouched.

"In a bit. I promised Archie a few photos ASAP."

"But we have all day." I stabbed an innocent piece of chicken and tore it off the fork.

"You maybe have all day, but I need to get this done. Your place is stunning in the afternoon sun, and I'd like a few great shots to display on my webpage." She nodded to herself and quickly reorganized one shelf of titles.

"But you didn't decorate this house. You gave me the colour scheme and that was about it."

She spun around and laughed. "Yeah, because I

119

know what I'm doing. It's the colour choice of the bookshelves and the couch colours that make it uber inviting and yet rustic and beach ready."

"That sounds like one too many ideas rolled into one thought." I pierced another bite of chicken.

She had the audacity to mock a shocked expression. "I've won dozens of awards for my skills, and I have a certain eye for things."

That was true. Her award list was long and prestigious, and her skills had been shown off in many celebrity's homes, especially those who use Vancouver as a temporary hub from Los Angeles.

"You know what, just finish whatever photos you need to take. I'll be outside." I swiped my plate off the counter and stormed out to the beach, dragging a camping chair with me. With one hand, I kicked it open and flopped down in an instant, half expecting Beth to come and join me.

Really, at this point in my life, I should've known better. Beth didn't come out. At least not for a while. I wanted my friend here, not the elite designer. That had been part of my insistence at nagging her to visit. Last night, I was upset and cranky with how things went between Eric and I, and the whole unknown with Parker. More than anything else, I just needed my friend.

By the time Beth did grace me with her presence,

my lettuce had wilted, and my chicken likely wasn't safe to eat.

She walked over, in her stocking feet and stood in front of me. "What's up with you? You've been a total bitch since I landed."

"Nothing." I hung my head. "And everything."

"Want to start at the beginning and tell me about it?" She lowered herself to stare into my eyes like she used to in our college days.

"I think it's this place." I waved my hands around.

"Oh yeah, the beach, the views, you're right, it's awful." There was a wisp of a smile in her good-natured tone. "Come back to the house and talk to me. Come see what I've done." She patted my hand and grabbed my plate.

I dragged my chair back and left it at the bottom of the stairs, ascending with some apprehension. Beth was practically cheerful, so she did something wild.

My jaw hit the floor. Somehow, she pulled it off. My place looked like a full-sized magazine spread. Everything had been rearranged, and there were new items I wasn't familiar with. Yes, it looked wonderful, but it wasn't my home anymore – it lacked my personal touch. Even my kitchen had been transformed, ready for a family of four to sit and have breakfast. How in the hell did she do that?

"I can see by your wonder, that you are impressed."

It wasn't even a question, just puffing out her chest in self-praise.

"Did you get all your pictures taken?"

"I sure did. They're great, and Archie loves the teasers I've sent."

"It does look ready to house a family, or even a couple just starting retirement. It looks prim and proper."

She beamed as she waltzed around. "And this is why I get paid the big bucks. I can work with what you have, add a few personal props, and bam. Knockout city. Isn't it beautiful?"

"It's…" I didn't have the right words. "Wow."

"Damn right it is."

My eyes went to the ceiling. "What about upstairs?" My curiosity was piqued. What changes had she made?

"Well, it's not the heart of the home, but I did manage a few pictures. I didn't stage those, just worked off the very basics you have up there. In order to be worthy of a page spread, it needs a complete overhaul, and I didn't bring enough for that. However, for a market listing, it's perfect." She laughed. "Have I mentioned it needs more greenery for a splash of colour? It's very shades of white and grey."

Nodding, I ran my hand over the table I'd recently painted, now set for four with three candles in the centre.

"So, tell me what's going on with you because I so want to tell you what's going on with me." In her first truly caring gesture, she pulled me over to the couch and sat beside me.

"I don't even know where to begin."

"Well, let's start with the guy who's breaking your heart."

I fell back and leaned into the softness. "It's complicated. When I first got here, he remembered me, but my past life, if you will, didn't faze him. We hung out, enjoyed each other's company–"

Beth was practically twitching beside me. "Get to the good stuff. The rest of this is boring. Blah, blah, blah. Did you make out?"

I stared incredulously.

"Oh my god, you did. That's wonderful. So, what's the problem?"

She was jumpy with anticipation, but it wasn't because she actually wanted to hear about Eric, she wanted me to finish so *she* could talk. Nothing ever changed with her. My heart broke a little seeing my friend in a new light.

"I still need to figure out what the problem is." I leaned back further into seat and rubbed my tummy, feeling a slight movement as the baby shifted. "Tell me what's up with you. You're just all lit up."

"Well, it all has to do with Archie."

"Your realtor friend?"

"You should remember from long ago, we started as business partners where I'd stage the houses he was selling, and one thing led to another. His business grew, mine hit the roof exponentially and I started my own company, which you know, has taken off and the most elite of executives and celebrities have me stage their homes."

I smiled, very much aware of my friend's success. She was the little engine that could.

"And the two of you just signed on to do the Canadian version of *Property Brothers*?"

She inhaled and folded her hands on her lap. "Nope. Lily, he proposed."

My jaw hit me in the chest with a drop and I swallowed to bring it back. "You're engaged?"

"As of Thursday."

I scanned her hand, looking for the ring.

"Oh, yeah, that." She crossed her legs and gave me a chagrin. "Well, it wasn't really me, so we're searching for a new one."

"You didn't like the one he proposed with?"

Deep down, I knew Beth was a trite materialistic, but how you turn down a ring someone picked out for you? Who does that?

"Didn't like it? Gawd, it was awful." She batted her hand through the air as if she were batting away a bad memory. "Anyways, so we're going shopping tomorrow afternoon when he picks me up from the airport. Going to go check out the higher end stores, as I'm sure there'll be something more my style."

I plastered a fake smile, hating myself just a little while I did it. "That's fantastic. I'm so happy for you. Never thought I'd see the day when you'd decide to walk the aisle."

Years ago, she'd claimed marriage was too time consuming, and it would threaten her time and energy on becoming the best and most well-known designer. Guess since she'd already nailed the last part, she could devote time to a marriage.

"So, my next big question is…" She inhaled and held her breath for a second. "Will you be my Maid of Honour?"

My first reaction was a hard no, as there was no way I'd be able to be the kind of help she needed, and truth be told, having watched her at studio photo shoots, all I could picture was a bridezilla. Still, what kind of a friend turns that down?

"You have to think about this? Figured you'd be all over it?"

Think, Lily, think. "Well, with the baby and everything…" I wasn't lying, and I wasn't being a bad friend.

"Oh, don't worry." Her shoulders relaxed and her features softened. "We're thinking we'll need a minimum of a year, maybe even two or three years to plan the wedding of the century, so you have lots of time to lose the weight." She patted my stomach for good measure.

I snorted. "That wasn't my first concern, but thanks."

"Lil, you're carrying a baby. Of course, you're going to put on weight. Your face is so much rounder than it was a month ago when you left."

It didn't feel rounder, but my hands touched my cheeks just the same. I pushed myself to a stand and moved around. Two to three years was a long way away, lots could happen in that time. "You know what, sure. I'll do it." I nodded my head and agreed to the position, unsure of what that would entail at this point.

"Sure? Wow." Her lips curled into a sneer. "Thanks for the enthusiasm. A month ago, you would've been all over that."

"A month ago, I was a different person."

She threw her hands in the air and punched her finger in my direction. "I knew coming here would change you. I knew it was a bad idea right from the start. I said it many times to Archie. *She's going to move back there, and she'll be different. She'll lose her edge.* And look at you. I was so right; it makes me sick."

She narrowed her eyes and popped up onto her feet. "You've gone soft. Before you were hard core, a go-getter, and now you're falling apart."

I crossed my arms over my chest. "I'm not falling apart, *we've* fallen apart."

"We?"

"Yeah. We're two different people, living two very different lives."

"That's not true and you know it."

"Isn't it?" My hands fell to my side in defeat. "Tell me something I've shared with you since I've moved back here. I know, better yet, tell me the name of the guy I'm interested in."

She took a step back. "You've never mentioned his name, because I would've remembered."

"I have. At least three times." I wanted to add *you've even met him,* but that would be giving her too big a hint and I wanted to make my point.

"Well, you don't know anything about me."

She stood there, in total silence, while I listed off all the things about her, and those were just the recent ones I'd learned in my absence.

My voice softened as my heart tore a little. "Face it, Beth, we've grown apart. It happens to the best of friends and it's happening to us. I can't keep up with your lifestyle, and you know what, that's okay."

127

Tears streamed down her cheeks, and I hesitated. In the years I've known Beth, crying wasn't something I'd ever witnessed, and I wasn't sure if she was angry or truly upset by the truth.

Instead, she took a sharp breath and moved around the living room, gathering her items, and shoving them under her arms. Her stomps sounded up the stairs, and a door slam followed.

Guess she was angry.

Chapter Thirteen

My supper remained largely untouched as I sat on my back deck, finishing up an email. Beth's angry stomps crossed back and forth over my head while she packed her things, and readied to leave, but with no car and no flight leaving until the morning, she was stuck. Maybe that was okay, because I wasn't really wanting her to leave, we both needed a cooling off though.

From under the cover of darkness, Eric hauled out a couple of chairs and a stack of wood, getting a crackling bonfire under way. One by one, my island friends arrived, first Willow and Arlo, with his guitar, followed by neighbour Jesse, who helped bring the fire to life. Eventually Mitch and Cedar arrived, her infectious giggle echoing between the houses.

Between the twang of Arlo's strumming, the smell of roasted hotdogs, and a bag of potato chips crinkling as it was passed around, a dull ache formed in my heart. But it was the laughter that truly did me in. The sweet snorts from Cedar as Mitch shared a story I didn't quite understand were like a current under the water, it pulled on my heartstrings, tempting me to join in the fun.

I tried to remain inconspicuous, but on a quick run to the house, Eric spotted me hiding in the shadows.

"Hey." He stepped closer to my deck but maintained a safe distance. "You're welcome to come and join the party, you know?"

"I know." But I really felt I shouldn't. After last night, maybe hanging out with Eric wasn't the smartest idea.

"Where's your friend?"

"Sulking in her room." I deadpanned. "I think we're breaking up."

Eric cocked his head and ran his hands through his hair, before walking onto the deck and grabbing the chair nearest me. "You okay?"

"I'll get over it." My body sagged and my gaze wandered over to the fire, watching the occasional spark shoot into the air with a pop.

Now, I wasn't really upset over the loss of friendship, since deep down I'd maybe seen it coming. Perhaps it was karma coming back to slap me in the face, destined to be alone in life, as a payback for being so bad.

Thinking about all my past crimes, tears slipped freely and streamed down my cheeks, cooling as the ocean air breezed past me.

I sniffed.

He wrapped his hand around mine. "You're clearly not okay."

What I really wanted was to cradle into someone and feel arms wrapped around me, whispering how everything would be fine, but that was never my reality. "Coming back here has been a real eye opener, more than I expected. I wanted a change of scenery, to think through my life, and instead of all that, I realized it wasn't a change I needed, it was insight. I met you, or got reacquainted with you," I wiped away my river, "and it seemed like you accepted me for me. And I'd been looking for that for so long that I didn't understand it had happened, until it was taken away from me."

He shifted in his seat and gave my hand a gentle squeeze. "I never left you."

"You did. Yesterday, after we did it." Where yesterday I'd been on top of the world, now I had shame over our experience.

"Listen, about that." Before I went to open my mouth, he covered it with his finger. "You're going to hear what I have to say." There was a gentle finality to his words. "Yesterday was one of the best days I've had in a long time, and because of that, it also scared me to a whole new level I wasn't expecting." He still held my hand, but his head hung as his shoulders rolled in. "I haven't been entirely truthful with you."

My eyes widened as I stared.

"Like you said, I do have a story; I just don't like to share it. I'm envious of you as you don't hold anything back, and when you unloaded about Jordan and your crazy past, my heart went out to you, and I want to be as honest with you as you are with me."

I squeezed his hand. "Whatever you want to share, I'll never tell."

His chest vibrated with a sigh and he twisted away from me, checking out the fire.

I understood the need to make sure a private moment stayed private.

"People are never truly how they present themselves to the world, and I just got tired of the constant lies." He shook his head. "And it's not just hiding an illness from your social media accounts, or anything like that. It's the illusion of perfection and an utter fakeness. It's too much." A long, lingering sigh breeze out of him.

"The last few attempts at a relationship have revealed a different persona than the person they pretend to be to complete strangers. Where's the honesty? Where's the vulnerability? Why do women have to project this ideal of being a size zero, when it's all smoke and mirrors?" His voice had a haunting lilt to it, and his words were soft and distant. "This one girl I was seriously into, she'd wake up before me, sneak out of bed and reapply her makeup and brush her teeth, so when I rolled over, she was already perfect looking. Sure, maybe for the first few dates, it's fine or whatever, but she refused to let me see her in her raw and natural state even after a few months. It just got to be too much. We'd go out and she pretended to be this warm and generous person, but the second the door closed to the outside world, she was spewing nastiness."

He sighed, and his voice drifted off as if trapped in a memory he needed to work through before it'd let go of him. "The last girl I dated; things were super serious. She was a B list celebrity, working in Vancouver, but based in LA. Her social media pics showcased her flawless beauty, but it was all lies. She was gorgeous without all the clown makeup."

I rubbed my fingertips over my face. Not sure I'd refer to it as clown makeup, but I never left the house without a bit of mascara and some colour on my lips.

"Her twitter platform boasted of her charitable causes, one of which… well, let's just say behind closed doors, it was the polar opposite. Learning how she really was versus her portrayed image, it terrified me. It made me start to wonder if I'd ever find someone whose outside beauty matched their inside beauty." He snapped out of his reverie and stared at me. "Until you arrived."

I focused on him, his beautiful silhouette against the backdrop of a glowing, rusty-coloured fire, sparks shooting out in all directions.

"When I first arrived, people talked, and I let them have their glory. They were just words, and they didn't know me, or know what I'd been through. It's exhausting on a whole other level trying to be someone you're not, but here, I was me. Laid back, happy to walk around with my hair messed to get the mail." He covered his mouth in mock horror. "But after time, the gossip faded. I gave them no fuel for their fire."

My voice lowered to a barely audible whisper and I pulled away from him and crossed my legs. "I wish I could be like that and not have the whispers bother me as much. And no offence, dating a high-profile celebrity and being there when someone jumped to his death are two different things."

A shudder rolled down my body, like a wave on the beach.

"But you are innocent. You were not responsible for Jordan's death. This town knows it, you're just an outlet for their misplaced anger and in time, they'll see how wonderful you are." He stretched out an arm and wiped away a small trail of my tears. "And truly, if they can't see that, then it's on them. Not you. You've paid for your mistakes, and you've moved on."

He had a point, however… "But yesterday, you brought them up." Hurt coursed through my veins. Things had been going so well too.

He held his head in his hands. "Yeah, and for that, I'm beyond sorry. I wasn't bringing the past up to hurt you." The tiny fray on the edge of his shorts grew as he tugged and pulled on a few of the loose threads. "It was me trying to verbalize my thoughts, and I screwed up by leading off and using that as an example. I wanted to tell you how we're the same, even though we're different." His breathing increased as the clouds breezed by. "But my feelings muddled everything up, and I got so confused."

"You've mentioned that." I recrossed my legs and rubbed my belly as I leaned back. This chair was no longer comfortable, and I needed to stand and stretch.

"Thing is I…" He shifted in his seat and reached for my hand. "I have feelings for you, but you keep saying you're not here for a long time, so it's been hard for me to move forward, to not push us forward together."

Yes, that would make things confusing. "I'm sorry."

"And after this afternoon, it got me thinking if I could handle it. You, the baby, and you know, more."

My heart pounded with every word and breath he

took, my eyes searching his as the bonfire behind him blurred.

"And I do want it all, but I know I can't. You're leaving soon, and I've struggled with holding back my feelings because you've made me crave it all. You and the baby, even though I know it's not possible as I can't live in the city again." Ripples of electricity bolted up my legs when his fingertips grazed my knee.

"It makes me happy to hear you say that." More tears slipped from their holds. "I can't either."

"What?"

I smeared dampness across my cheeks. "When I was in the city, I was like Beth, or I had to be since I hung out with her and thought she was a superstar as I channeled that energy and personality into my business. But when she landed, and was acting well, like herself, it came across to me like she was being a total bitch." I lowered my voice, even though I didn't need to, I was pretty sure Beth was upstairs thinking the same about me, or at least, telling Archie as much. "I knew something changed. I no longer wanted to be that person. When my life fell apart, it was actually a blessing in disguise, I just didn't see it until today." I twisted in my chair to look him deep in the eyes. "Even though this town hates me..."

"They don't hate you."

I tipped my head from side to side, occasionally

watching my island friends. The laughter had died down, and there was no more singing and guitar playing.

"Yeah, they do, but that's okay. I know I can live with it, or at least learn to try. It's a reminder of who I was. And me remembering that maybe isn't a terrible thing because it'll keep it from ever happening again." I uncrossed my legs and scooted closer. "Eric, I really like you. I love being around you, and I want to stay here with you. I have no intentions of going home."

"The hell you aren't!"

The hairs on the back of my neck sprung to attention and my breath lodged in the back of my throat.

Parker.

Chapter Fourteen

O ut of the shadows, my former boyfriend showed himself. "Parker, what the hell are you doing here?"

I jumped to my feet, but not as fast as Eric, who stood in front of me.

"Your ex, I take it?" He whispered out the side of his mouth.

"Unfortunately."

"Unfortunately? Really?" Parker moved closer, but his features turned sinister in the mix of light and shadows. Enough to cause the hairs to remain standing.

"What are you doing here?" I swallowed down a lump of budding fear. Never in our entire relationship had I had reason to feel threatened by him, but my whole body was on alert regardless. "How did you…"

"Find you?" He finished my question before I had a chance. "Easy. Beth has geo-tags on her pics."

I shot a glance up to the top floor where Beth was.

"She posted pictures to her IG account. It wasn't that hard to figure out, especially after hearing her talk to her secretary about flying to the island."

Parker was a gifted IT guy, that's how I knew how to turn off geo-tagging. He'd taught me on our second date.

"What do you want?"

"I came for you and the baby. It's time for you to come home."

Eric inhaled sharply and inched to the left to cover me more.

I stepped around him. This was about my past. My indiscretions. My giant assed mistakes. "Parker, you left. You packed up your drawer and took off. I didn't hear from you for a week."

At least. Maybe more. I was more surprised he'd physically left than I was heartbroken about it.

"Well…" He tilted his head back as his arms gently swung by his sides. "I've had time to think and reassess my life. Sure, I'm young to be a father, but think about it. The kid and I can grow up together. I'll teach him all about The Avengers and Star Wars, and he can help me mature. It's a win-win situation."

Young would describe it. There were eight years between us, and he'd only graduated from university last year.

"I came here to make amends. To apologize and bring you back home. Your friends are waiting. They miss you. I've missed you."

I huffed. "Oh yeah?" The joke tickled me because it was really only Beth who had kept in contact. To the others, I'd gone crazy, and they never returned my calls or texts. I didn't believe for a nanosecond they missed me.

"They're worried about you, babe." His voice softened. "Come home."

There wasn't anything drawing me in that direction. Despite the rumours and whispers, I was much more at home here in Cheshire Bay than I was back in my trendy apartment. I belonged on the beach; it was part of my soul. And I wanted to make something of my life with Eric. He'd been saying the sweetest things moments before Parker's arrival.

"I'm not interested. In fact, I called a realtor, and the apartment is going on the market at the end of the month." I rubbed Eric's arm. "I'm staying here."

"The hell you are." His voice raised a full octave and echoed between mine and Eric's place.

Enough to attract attention, and the light from the bonfire flickered as the group walked towards my deck, with Mitch, Arlo, and Jesse in the lead.

"What's going on?" Mitch asked, his voice one of no nonsense.

Eric cleared his throat. "This is Lily's ex-boyfriend, who has tracked her down despite her refusal to see him."

"She's carrying my child. I have every right to be here."

"Bullshit." Eric's voice gathered strength. "You gave up that right when you walked away."

"But that's my DNA in her. She can't keep me away. The people on the internet said I have every right to see my child. To watch it being born, if I choose, and to be a part of its life."

"Actually..." I started speaking, but quickly snapped my jaw shut. One thing at a time.

Eric carried on. "Any man worth his salt would never abandon his baby or his baby momma. And you did by walking away like a god-damn coward."

"But I'm back."

Eric stepped off the deck, feet firmly in the sand. "Gather yourself a lawyer and plead your case to the courts. They'd love hearing about how you walked away when she needed you most. Oh, and to top it off, if you're not already paying child support, they will come after you and make sure you do. So, get your finances straightened out."

Parker stared up at me, one eye on the group to his left. "She can take care of me, right, Babe? You've always been my sugar momma."

I shivered, but not from the cold. Yes, I made more

than Parker, but after a couple of years, or five, he'd catch up in salary. Parker hadn't brought financial stability to the relationship.

He gave me his full attention. "Plus, you know how magical we are together. Sex between us was out of this world. We were banging, animalistic almost. Every girl since has been meh at best. But us?"

"Just shut up!" Suddenly, I wished the ground would open and swallow me whole.

Parker stepped closer and tossed his hands up in protest when Eric, Mitch, Arlo, and Jesse formed a line. "Look, all I want is to be with Lily and the baby." He gave me his full attention. "When I told Mom and Dad they were going to be grandparents, they were so excited. They bought us a crib, and a car seat, and so many clothes. They're so proud of me, and happy for us." He faced me completely, arms dangling to the side. "Lily, we can work out our problems. I can be the man you need me to be. Just tell me what you want, and I'll do it. I drove all this way to see you." He got down on bended knee and put his hands into a prayer formation.

I stepped closer to the edge of the deck, not wanting to get much closer, and wrapped my fingers around the lip of the railing. "Anything at all?"

Cedar stalked behind Eric and up the stairs to me, where she put her hand on mine.

Eric glanced up at me, confusion twitching across his face.

"Whatever you want, Babe. I'm at your mercy. I need you. The Bald Avenger–"

I threw up in my mouth.

"We need you."

For a heartbeat, I took in Eric's face. He was the one I wanted, not Parker. In all honesty, and as awful as it was, Parker wasn't that serious a boyfriend to me. We'd only been together less than a year, and he wasn't the one I saw a future with. He never had been. He'd been a placeholder at best. That's why I never officially let him move in, and he only had a drawer.

"I want you to go home, clear your things from my apartment, and return the key to the super. After that, I never want to see you again." I squared my shoulders and tipped up my chin.

Cedar rubbed my arm for moral support.

"Babe…" His voice nearly cracked, but he puffed it out in front of the three men staring down at him. "We can fix…"

"No, we can't. There's nothing to fix. You need to leave. Now."

Eric stepped forward. "Your time is up, Parker."

My ex's face cracked and for a breath, I worried he'd snapped. "For the rest of your life, you'll be tied to me. That baby connects us, and you can't keep me from him. Mom, Dad, and I'll see you in court." He pointed a finger in my direction.

"That's where you're absolutely wrong. This baby isn't yours."

A collective hush fell over the area and all eyes stared in my direction. My life was more fubar than they realized.

Chapter Fifteen

Parker's jaw dropped. "You're such a liar. I was there. The condom was destroyed." It was like he didn't even care there were others around.

Heat singed my cheeks as I did care. These people all standing around me were my friends, and it bothered me I was about to air more of my dirty laundry in front of them.

Inhaling sharply, I paused and looked at each them, stopping on Parker briefly, before taking in the clenched features on Eric's face.

"The baby isn't yours, Parker. When that happened, I was already pregnant." Newly pregnant, to be honest. The positive test was still in the trash.

"What?" He backed up and rubbed his legs, almost as if he were encouraging blood flow into them to run like hell. Which is probably what he should've done months ago.

"On my twenty-ninth birthday, well, actually, it was before that when I'd made up my mind…" I waved my hand through the air as if that would erase the messed-up words falling out of my mouth. "A while back," I said with more clarity, "I decided I wanted a baby, but not necessarily a man. Men tend to love me and leave me. Point in case."

I tipped my head to the side. Parker was a prime example.

I avoided all eye contact as I scanned the beach. Standing on my porch, the weight of their stares reduced me in size, and I felt as if I were trapped in the Jerry Springer show or something.

"I just wanted someone to love me as unconditionally as I would love it." Instinctively, my hand rubbed the top of my bump.

A sigh rolled out of Eric. At least I thought it was him.

"And a baby was the answer. I was more than prepared to raise it on my own. I am financially secure and had a great job…" As a former regional manager. "And I have a fantastic home to live in. So… I did what any reasonable person without a steady man in her life would do."

"You bought sperm?" The disgust was strong in his tone.

It sounded horrible when said like that. "Yes, in a way. I selected a candidate, based on intelligence and some other figures that would probably make you all think even less of me than you do already. I'd made that decision long before you entered the picture."

Cedar's hand squeezed my shoulder. "I think it's great. I think you're amazing."

It warmed my heart to hear that. Being a single mother came with enough stigma, but I was terrified when they learned I did it on purpose, it would be even worse. "Thanks for saying that," I whispered to Cedar.

To the waiting crowd standing there with shock on their faces, but hadn't yet as a group disbanded, I added, "I'd been having regular appointments, and the timing was right, so I went in for insemination. And it took." I pushed at a little foot digging into my ribs. For the rest of his or her life, they would know how much they were wanted. It was no accidental pregnancy.

"And me? Did you just use me for sex?" Parker had every right to be hurt and had the shoe been on the other foot, I know I would've been too.

I shrugged. "Well..." The sex wasn't as great as Parker claimed, at least not from my viewpoint, however, it was nice to have someone to chat with about Star Wars movies and have a little warmth in my bed. "At some point, yes. But truth be told, I expected you to walk away from us before I needed to say anything. You and I weren't really serious, and I felt you knew that."

"Wow. Thanks a lot."

"I'm sorry. You were..." My inner bitch was fighting to be freed, but I needed to control her escape. I inhaled and held my breath for a second. "You were a way to pass time. I didn't see us in the long-term future. And you didn't either. We had more disagreements about the littlest things than most people do in thirty years."

"Wow." He stumbled backwards and sent me a long, painful glance before he broke eye contact. "For real? You got knocked up in a clinic? It's not my baby?"

"I have the documentation to prove it."

"Wow." He snorted and rubbed his face. "Just one more thing. Did you ever really love me?"

My gaze fell to the railing I gripped with all my strength. No matter what had happened between us, I didn't dare say the word that would possibly destroy him. Instead, I focused on breathing to match the roll of the waves – the only other audible sound.

"Well, fuck me." It came out in a whisper but grew in strength. "You know what, fuck you! Fuck you for playing with my heart like that, you bitch." He pointed to Eric. "You called me the coward, but who's the coward now? She wouldn't even fess up, until push came to pull, that it wasn't my child. She's the coward. I knew I'd done

148

the right thing when I walked away. You can bet your sweet ass, I won't be coming back. Now we're through."

Parker retreated between the houses and stopped. His voice cracked. "I thought you were different. Damn. You broke my heart, bitch. Rot in hell, you whore."

Eric and his friends stood there as Parker stormed to his car and squealed the tires as he pinned it.

It didn't matter that he was gone, his words ripped open my heart. All this time, I'd been the one who'd done the hurting. I should've been upfront with him. When he left, I figured it was for the best, and he was right, I did take the cowardly way out by keeping my lips shut. Damn.

Cedar rubbed my back, which was now aching from standing in an awkward and tightened position. "I think you're incredible to have a baby on your own. To *want* a child without needing a man to support you."

A weak smile crossed my face. I certainly didn't feel incredible. Not at this moment.

"Are you okay?" Willow asked as she approached the deck.

"I'm fine, thank you. Just a little achy."

"Have a seat." She helped me into a chair but stood abruptly when Eric returned and breezed onto my deck.

"He's gone." He leaned against the banister after he climbed the stairs. "Will that be the last we see of him?"

I nodded. "As much as I just broke his heart, Parker

doesn't mess with documentation. It's the be-all and end-all for him. He's a huge collector of comic things and if stuff doesn't have the required paperwork to claim its legitimacy, he's not interested."

I tucked my hair behind my ear as I lowered my head. "I'm sorry you had to see all that. And to learn even more nasty information about me."

"Cedar, I think we should head back to the fire." Willow grabbed her hand and led her away from Eric and me.

"Bonfire time," Mitch declared after giving a nod to his best friend. "Come join us soon, you two."

Eric inhaled and exhaled and scuffed his foot on the floorboards. "Was that the truth?"

I gazed up. "Yeah."

"You really think men love you and leave you?" The pitch in his voice was hard to deny.

"I really do." The cold hard truth stung.

"And you're still planning to stay here in Cheshire Bay?"

There was no place else I wanted to be. "Yes." The word was stronger than anticipated.

"Answer me honestly, if you and I were to start things, you believe with your whole being, that I will somehow end it and walk away?"

Like a bad smell, it lingered in the air, but the truth

was the truth. Never once had a guy cared for me, or about me. I had no reason to believe a man falling in love with me was an option.

"You know what, don't answer that."

I swallowed and rubbed my bump. The little one was wide awake now.

"Of course, you're going to think that. You have nothing to argue against it because no man has been good enough."

"What?"

"So, from here on in, I plan on being that guy. The one who stands up for you, and who'll stand by you when the going gets tough. Who won't throw in the towel and find another when things don't go as planned, because in life, if it's one thing I can say with utter truth, it's that nothing ever goes as planned." He winked and bridged the distance between us, offering his hand.

I pulled myself to a stand, quivering in front of him. "That sounds like a mighty promise." My heart skipped a beat at the very idea of us being together for the long haul, especially since I knew in my soul he was the one I wanted.

He moved his finger as he spoke. "I cross my heart to be the man you need in your life. To be the sun in your day. To be the reason your heart flutters. I will prove to you how amazing you are, and how wonder and kindness are radiating out of you. I promise to tell you every day, even when you finally start believing that truth yourself."

Tears built impressively fast and busted over their dams even quicker. "Oh, Eric. I hope you mean all that."

"Every. Single. Word." He threaded his fingers through my hair and pulled me in for a kiss, hesitating for a second. "You make me the happiest guy in Cheshire Bay."

I pushed into him with all I had, feeling my legs weaken at the strength of his kiss, and the baby wiggling between us. Breaking apart, I gazed into his darkening eyes. "Perhaps you should get back to your friends."

"*Our* friends, and yes, let's." Eric linked his fingers through mine. "Let's go have a bite to eat and sing until the sun comes up."

I glanced quickly to the ceiling. Beth was up there. "First, I think I need to talk to someone. But it won't take long." I brushed my lips over his in parting. "Give me a few minutes."

He waited until I was inside my kitchen before he walked away. Squaring my shoulders, I braced myself for another battle and headed upstairs.

* * *

My knuckles rapped against Beth's door.

"Come in."

Twisting the knob, I opened it slowly and entered.

"Hey."

She sat at the head of the bed, phone in hand, but set it down as I approached. "What's up?"

"Listen, I'm sorry about what happened before." I smoothed out a wrinkle on the comforter before I sat at the foot of the bed.

Her frostiness was gone. "I just got a text from Archie. You're selling?"

My shoulders rolled inward, and I tucked my chin down. "Yeah, just not this place, sorry. I'm going to stay a while, see if I can't find myself, and find out where I truly belong."

Beth had packed all the extras she'd brought and returned my space back into what it was before her arrival. She sighed as she twisted the Pandora bracelet on her bony wrist and fiddled with the charms.

"I think we're both on edge; you with the change in your life, me in mine. We're going two different directions."

A crack in my serious façade formed, and a smile inched to the tip of my lips. "That we are. And that's okay because our friendship is strong enough to weather this storm." I fiddled with one of the throw pillows, holding it over my chest. "I was just in a bad place as the guy I was interested in didn't seem to let my past go, but it was a terrible misunderstanding on my part because I'm just highly sensitive. I'm trying to prove to this village how I've changed, and I take that negative energy personally, even if it's not there. I am deeply ashamed of who I was, and I regret my past."

"And that isn't a terrible thing, as you'll be able to make sure your little one doesn't act the same way. In that respect, it's a life lesson." Her hand settled on the top of my bump.

"Thanks for that." I offered her my hand, to which she squeezed. "When you breezed in and took over, it bothered me and made me wonder if I'd ever be able to take care of things myself."

"Oh, Lil. You are so much stronger than you think you are. Look at you. You're going to raise a child, on your own, in a totally rural area." Despite the words, there was a smile growing and pride in her eyes. "I'm in awe of you."

"Really? I'm the one who's in awe *of you*. You're a powerful woman, so determined and resourceful. Someone people respect." My vision blurred as I spoke. Why hadn't we had a civil conversation like this before? Now I was really going to miss my friend.

Beth must've been feeling the same thing as she burst into tears and scooted over to give me a hug. I can't remember the last time that happened. College maybe? "I crept out onto your balcony. I heard everything. I'm not the only determined woman in this room."

"Oh? You know Parker was here."

She tipped her chin down a little. "For that, I'm so sorry. What the hell is geo-tagging?" There was a weak laugh. "But you… you're amazing. And your friends? Lily, this is where you belong. Those are your people. They stood ready to battle, for you. The way the guys took the front and that one girl rushed on to the deck, well, I'm sorry to say, that never happened back home, did it?"

I shook my head. Usually, people scattered into the breeze.

"But here…" She rubbed my bello. "I hate to say it because I'm going to miss you so much, but this just isn't a place to live, this is your home."

My vision blurred further as I took in my best friend. "I'm going to miss you too." I embraced her in another hug and wiped away my own fallen tears. "I'm not that far a drive away, or a flight even. Besides, I'll be back for a few days in a couple of weeks to clear everything out."

She delicately dabbed her eyes with a tissue. "If Archie's selling, you won't mind if I stage it? I'd oversee it personally, and I won't even charge you."

"I'd love that." No doubt with her expertise, it would sell that much faster, and garner a higher profit.

"And what about the pictures I took here? Can I still use them in promotional materials?"

"Absolutely. Send me a release form, and I'll let

155

you use them on your website or however you see fit." She was a gifted designer, and it was her colour selection that made the main floor look so amazing.

"Thank you." She gazed around the room, bobbing her head. "This room will make an excellent nursery. Since you're staying, you need to go shopping."

"Only if you help me pick out furniture." I rose and ambled around the space. My former room was going to be a nursery. With a lock on the window when she got older.

She beamed from ear to ear as she got off the bed and smoothed out the indent. "As much as I want to jump all over that, I think there's someone else who should, at the very least, help you assemble it all if he doesn't help you pick it out first."

"Speaking of Eric, they're really hoping you'll come join us on the beach for songs and hot dogs."

"Oh, my favourites." Her eyes rolled but she chuckled good-naturedly. "Let me change and I'll be there."

I walked to the door and gave my bestie a solid once over. "One more thing…"

"What's that?"

Rather than speak, I stepped over to my friend and wrapped her in a full hug. "I love you."

"I love you too." She squeezed me tight. "Now go. Eric's waiting for you. I'll be five minutes tops."

With a spring in my step, I bobbed my way over to where my guy was and began what was the start of a new adventure.

Epilogue

"'m back. Sorry I'm late." Eric stepped into my house and came to the back deck. "Have I got some news for you. I just brought over a trip from Seattle…" He bent down in front of me. "What's up?"

I relaxed my grip on the chair and opened my eyes. "Contraction."

"Okay." If he was panicking, he gave no indication. "Have you been having them long?"

I tossed him my phone and he opened the app, bobbing his head from side to side. "That's not bad, a few hours, and they're still less than a minute long." Someone had paid attention at our last prenatal appointment. "Shall I call Willow?"

"Maybe just to update her, but she doesn't need to come right away."

A few weeks back, I'd agreed to meet with her after

I'd cleaned out my apartment. By time I flew home, I was hurting and having minor contractions, likely from stress and overexertion. Willow put me at ease instantly, and I couldn't get over how my body responded in her warmth and soothing presence. Arlo had been right, it was more than the physical aspect of pregnancy, she really cared about the person carrying the baby. After that, I signed up to be her patient, which made bonfire night a little tricky, but we'd both become good at not discussing the pregnancy then.

"What were you saying about your flight?" I gestured for his help to stand, and immediately bent over as another contraction rippled through my body. Squeezing his hand, I counted to ten and inhaled, counted to five and exhaled. It worked to take the edge off, but since I needed to breathe through them, my body was telling me I was in labour.

"Well, Mitch is going to have a hard night."

"Why's that?" I leaned against his muscled chest.

"The two passengers from Seattle were a mother and a child." He wrapped his arm around my waist and escorted me into the kitchen. "Are we setting up in here or upstairs?"

With Willow as my midwife, I was going to give birth in my home, I just needed to decide if I wanted the bedroom or the living room.

It was still early enough in the day, even though I knew labour could last well into the night. "The beach?"

"Really?"

"Just to labour, not give birth. For that we can come back inside. Somewhere." I squeezed his hand. "What about the mother and child?"

"Well, I didn't get all the details, but she's from Mitch's past and the guy was stone cold shocked."

I breathed hard and rested on the edge of the counter while Eric ran his hands over my back, up and across my shoulders. It was heavenly. Realization dawned on me about what he'd said about his passengers. "No…" I inhaled sharply as another contraction made an appearance. "And that's… Is it Mitch's child?"

"Appears so."

"Poor Cedar."

Eric laughed. "Poor Mitch."

I grunted. "Bobby from that construction place called…" Inhaling and exhaling, trying to get a grip on the surges. "The initial drawings… for Jordan… will be ready… on Monday."

A couple weeks back, I went to the mayor's office and practically begged to have something dedicated to Jordan. After some deliberation, and a quick vote to the council who eagerly welcomed the infusion of cash, there will now be a viewpoint named in his honour. The dedication ceremony won't happen until the spring, but the ball was rolling on selecting the appropriate monument or plaque.

"You know what," I panted, unable to focus on Eric as much as I wanted. "Call Willow, please, and give her an update. I need to go outside."

I slowly waddled my way back out onto the deck, into the mild September air as the giant bowling ball nestled between my legs threatened to push out at any moment. The towel hanging over the railing now became a squeeze toy as I tightened my grip around the edges while taking a stair at a time. I wanted my feet in the ocean.

Eric jumped off the deck and caught up. "She said she'll pop by in a spell to check on you."

"Great, thank you."

I made my way to the edge of the beach where the ocean kissed the sand. I threw the towel on the ground, a few feet from the shoreline in a crumpled mess which Eric quickly straightened out. Slowly, I lowered myself to the ground, not wanting to sit on my butt at all. Another grunt and I managed to roll over onto my forearms with my ass in the air.

"This will look awkward to the others down the beach."

"It'll give them something new to talk about."

Plus, I really didn't care. The position worked

wonders on my aching back, until another contraction hit. I rocked back and forth on my hands and knees, moaning, and shaking. When it passed, I put my head back on the towel.

While the sun made its decent toward the edge of the ocean, a couple dozen more contractions controlled my body and something deep inside changed on the last one.

"Eric?"

"Right here." But he sounded so far away, as if he were back at the house and I was all alone.

"It's happening."

"Here?" His voice cracked. "Okay, no worries. Just breathe. Let's get back to the house and up to the bed. Willow should be here by now."

A surge swelled within me, and I rocked back on my hands and knees, but it wasn't helping. I dropped my butt onto my heels and grunted. "Eric! Eric! Oh no!"

"Oh no, what?"

"He's… coming." I gripped Eric's shirt at the shoulders and pulled him close, digging my forehead into his pecs. "Eric…" And a strange, involuntary grunt tore out of my throat.

"Oh, it's baby time I see." A friendly voice spoke through my haze and dropped down beside me. "Honey, I'm going to need to remove…"

Eric moved quickly and stood behind me, holding

me under my arms.

An involuntary urge forced my body to push as Willow lowered my shorts. "Okay, Lily, the baby's head is right here. A gentle pant and it'll all be over. Good work."

"It's right there?" Eric asked, repositioning himself to hold me up.

"Lily, go ahead." Willow folded herself onto her knees and grabbed something from her bag.

"Oh! Oh!" A scream threatened to tear me apart, but I remembered from a prenatal meeting to channel that energy and push it down. A giant grunt consumed me, and a moment later, my baby was born.

"Congratulations."

Eric kissed my cheek. "Look at your baby."

I opened my eyes and searched between the baby's legs before I pulled him up into my arms and snuggled him against my chest, while tears of joy streamed down my cheeks as I took in my son.

Deep in my heart, I knew instantly what his name was going to be. Gazing down upon my father's namesake, I whispered his name. "Hi, Henry."

Willow gathered the towel under me. "Do you feel you can move back up to the deck?"

I inhaled sharply and nodded, guessing the distance to be less than twenty feet. Slowly, the four of us shuffled our way to the deck, where I tenderly sat down on a thick towel. Kissing my son's sweet head, and with tears still lingering in my eyes, I looked over at Eric, who knelt beside me. "Thank you."

"You did all the work."

"Thank you for welcoming me home when I first arrived, and for loving me the way you do." I reached to kiss him. "Thank you for accepting us."

"I couldn't dream of loving anyone more." He kissed me back and tenderly placed a sweet peck on my baby's head.

Moving to Cheshire Bay had been the best decision I'd ever made. The second best was giving my heart to Eric.

More Fabulous Reads

For the most up-to-date listings, please check the website:
www.hmshander.com

Dear Reader

The Cheshire Bay series has been one of the most fun series I've written. I've enjoyed spending my time there, and drawing up the maps, creating the family trees, and picturing the completely fictional town. Why can't Cheshire Bay be real?

Keep reading the series and learn more about Lily, Cedar, Amber, Mona, Iris, Summer, Chloe, Erin and Libby and their personal journeys to growth and love.

Would you like to be the first to know of upcoming releases, see the covers before anyone else, and just have all the insider information? Then you'll want to join my twice-a-month mailing list. Connect through my website – www.hmshander.com. I promise not to spam you, and I keep things fun with freebies and a scavenger hunt. Your time is valuable, and I appreciate how you've spent time reading my story (thank you for that!).

Finally, if you don't mind, I'd love a review on your favourite retailer site for Return to Cheshire Bay. It doesn't have to be long, even just as simple as "Eric is my new book boyfriend" works. Reviews and ratings help me gain visibility, and as I'm sure you can tell, reviews are tough to come by. Thank you so much for spending time with me.

Yours,

H.M. Shander

acknowledgements

If one good thing came out of the pandemic in 2020, it was these books – I'm absolutely in love with this series and all the characters. They are each unique, but together, they form a beautiful series, if I do say so myself.

I'm in awe of being able to do what I love, and to fulfill my dream, but writing these thanks yous never gets easier. Never. Always afraid I'll miss someone, or a category will be left out. And then I wonder, does anyone even read these? I know as an author, I do, but I wonder if readers do? Anyways, writing a book for the most part, is a solo endeavor, but I could not have this ready for you to read if not for the cheerleading and support of some magnificent people in my life.

First – my Shander family, whom you may know on my social media platforms as Hubs, The Teen, and Little Dude. Thank you from the bottom of my heart for letting me pursue what I love doing, for something that allows me to transport myself to another time and place – the summer of 2020 was a particular straining time, and you gave me this golden escape into the pages. For that, I'll be forever grateful, and if this series does well, we're going to do something incredible. Like really big and fun. Thank you for cheerleading as I had a sale, and watching the numbers climb. Thank you for encouraging me to keep going and to chase my dreams, and for the nonstop coffees I sometimes needed when I was on a role. I love you all with my whole heart.

To my parents and in-laws and extended family – Thank you for your support, and encouraging your friends and family to give my books a try. Having you visit me at markets and book signings means the world. I have an amazing family, and every day I'm thankful to you all. Thanks for being you.

To my wonderfully dedicated alpha reader – Mandy. My trusted go-to writing pal, the one who reads the first cleaned up draft. Where would I be without your support and guidance? Probably still cowering in a corner. Your comments and feedback are vital to me. I never have to wait long, and before I know it, my inbox has a response, and 99% of the time, your advice is bang on. I'm so glad we're in this business together, and you know I'm your biggest fan and cheerleader! You're going to go big, and I'm tagging along on the ride. You deserve the very best.

To my critique partner – Josephine. Thank you for spending your free time reading my words and pointing out what didn't make sense and what needed to be expanded on. How many times did I redo that opening chapter in Return? LOL, and Awake? You had your work cut out with that, eh? But, as always, your insight was invaluable, and the stories are better with your touch! Thank you.

To my beta readers – Shauna, Melissa, and Dawn. Thank you for cheering for the good, highlighting the bad, and letting me know what worked and what needed more explanation. Your feedback and insight are a gift I cherish.

To my cover designer – Eleanor. Great job! I'm super thrilled with how well all the covers turned out, including the special edition print cover! I simple adore all of them and can't stop staring! I'm so blessed to have discovered your talents, and I look forward to many more covers designed by you.

To my editor – Irina. Thanks for your dedication to fixing my errors and highlighting the inconsistencies. I think I'm getting better, right? At least it's not the same corrections every time. Heh-heh.

If I missed you, it certainly wasn't intentional. I know I couldn't be where I am without the help of so many others. Thank you! And thank you for reading and making it all the way to the end. You all rock.

about the author

USA TODAY bestselling author H.M. Shander is a star-gazing, romantic at heart who once attended Space Camp and wanted to pilot the space shuttle, not just any STS – specifically Columbia. However, the only shuttle she operates in her real world is the #momtaxi; a reliable electric car that transports her two kids to school and various sporting events. When she's not commandeering Elektra, you can find the elementary school librarian surrounded by classes of children as she reads the best storybooks in multiple voices. After she's tucked her endearing kids into bed and kissed her trophy husband goodnight, she moonlights as a contemporary romance novelist; the writer of sassy heroines and sweet, swoon-worthy heroes who find love in the darkest of places.

If you want to know when her next heart-filled journey is coming out, you can follow her on Twitter (@HM_Shander), Facebook (hmshander), or check out her website at www.hmshander.com.

Thanks for reading– all the way to the very end.